Death of the God
(*Or, The Book Eh-Eh_Ehh*)

By
Stanley Alexander MARTIN

Usable and safe operating manuals for consumer goods

A guideline

All rights reserved in equal parts by the partners of the SecureDoc project.
Version 1.0, printed in 2004

Disclaimer: This information is of a general nature and is not legal advice. Neither the project partners nor any person acting on behalf of these Institutions/Organisations is responsible for the use that might be made of the information.

Copyright 2008 Nana baBa jaH-aYe
ISBN: 978-0-9559904-4-1

Dedicated to The_God….

Several parts of this book was in "Death of the God", 2001, sponsored by Mind and The Millenium Commission....

CONTENTS....

i   Introduction

ii   a male beauty

iii   The Book Eh-Eh

iii   The Book of Death

INTRODUCTION....

Form contents mythics

Follows Go! Translator

ma	=	mother
pa	=	father
nana	=	grandparent
sah	=	chief
baas	=	Ruler
ra	=	spirit/sun…
ra-rah	=	*high spirit*
ra-ra-ra	=	*god*
ga	=	*gOd*
gah	=	*God….*
fi	=	for/mine
a	=	I/one/have
O	=	me/black one
oo!	=	wonderful
oh-oh	=	dangerous
ah-ah	=	lovely
a Oo	=	I am a powerful being
aha	=	I understand
nana a ra	=	My grandmother is a queen
a fi-wi baas	=	This is our ruler
e' eh-eh	=	He/She's actively acting like a high god
e' awe-awe	=	He/She's the biggest type of person

Deep-structured language

- Oo   a   ah   awe   a-awe…

- oo-awe oo-awe awe-awe….

a   ha   aha   aha-ah   aha-aha   *a-a-aha…*
a-a-a-aha   *a-a-a-a-aha*   *a-a-a-a-a-aha….*

e'   ee   ee-ee   e-e-e   e-e-e-e   e-e-e-e-e…
e-e-e-e-e   *e-e-e-e-e-e*   *e-e-e-e-e-e-e….*

e'   eh   eh-ee   eh-eh   awe…
a-awe   *oo-awe*   *oo-awe*   *awe-awe….*

fi-mi   fi-yu   fi-s/he/it fi-wi   fi-you   *fi-dem…*
fi-oonu   *fi-awe*   *fi-gah….*

i.

a-Ha?

Do you understand?

ii.

aHa - a-ha!

I understand!

1.

Akwaaba!
Welcome!

a-ha goo-goo aha…
A boo-boo?

Na! Fi-mi a-mi….

A yu fi-mi a-mi tu?

Aye!

2.

A li in me bed ana sleep:
A dream:

"One banana, too banana!"

A wek up!

One banana!

"Wey mi ada banana gone?"

A nahm e in me sleep!

3.

E fi-yu?

Look so…

Na!

Is fi-mi muma?

Look so….

Na!

Is fi-mi pupa?

Look so....

Na!

Is fi-mi!
Is fi-mi <u>nose</u>!

4.

Fi-mi nana baas!

Is fi-yu nana baas?

Aye...

Gad is Big Baas!

Yu know?

5.

Clap hands
Clap hands...

Gie thanks
Gie thanks
Clap hands...

...Thank you!....

6.

Shake hands
Shake hands....

Hello, I'm Stan
Hello
How are you?

I'm fine….

7.

Look dey
Look dey
A mek a face
      -   look dey!

A goo-goo gone!
A boo-boo dey dey!

8.

Goo-goo!
Sun is shining
Don't mek me a face
Mek me a smile!

Look dey now!
A goo-goo dey dey!

9.

<u>Outside</u>…
Sun is shining…
<u>Oo</u> e hot!

Day is snowing…
<u>Brr</u> e cold!

Day e rain…
<u>Al</u> me wet!

<u>Inside</u>…
<u>Oo-oo</u>….

A male beauty

"O!":
Storms*faith*
Mythic Form contents

-a concrete re-Construction-
(after
the risen sun:
ecOlogy myth,
Male-ism,
Egyptology,
Plato,
Pythagoras,
Hegel,
de Moivre,
Darwin,
Freud,
de Saussure,
Heisenstein,
Propp,
Levi-Strauss,
Lacan,
Barthes,
Stack Sullivan,
Williams,
Laing,
Derrida,
and, Feminism,
jaH-aYe:
the fallen night....)

"0": Content forms mythics
The myth of the male beauty gOd aDonis

-a concrete re-Construction-
(after Raymond Williams)

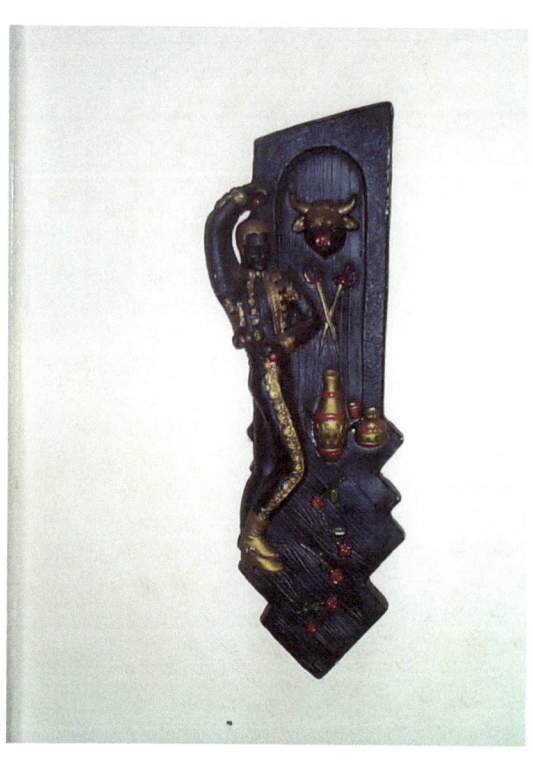

0: Structures of: *"myth"*

mythics...
i.   *a risen sun:*
       summer noon

F +(1/0) :~ F +(iNfinity)
    the River waxeth...

ecology myth
ii.:   *(after religion)*

F (1/0) ~ "1" ~ F (oNe-iNfinity)

Male
a: *after Male egO)*

$F -(-i. -i) :\sim F -(1/i)(1/i) :\sim F -(i^3)(i^3) :\sim F -(i^4)(i^2) :- a$ "1" = "too"...

Hieroglyphics
b: *(after Egyptology)*

"0" : pTaH
"00": nU
"0!": ThOth
"1": Ra
"2": Osiris

an iNfinity of "one"...

and: "the lack"...
c: *(after Feminism)*

$F -(i. i) \sim F (i^2)(i^2) :\sim F (i^3)(i) :- a$ "1"...

And: the thesis...
d: *(after Jah-ale)*

Beauty male: female
      :~ contradiction : nexus
perhaps ! :~ iNfinity
          : divine

as gOd :~ male/female : male
-iNfinity : "1" : + iNfinity :~ too...

key −inFINITY := +InFINITY
    AS WHERE IS "1"?
IF "1" : (i^2)

Lim 1/0 :∼ -iNfinity

Lim: 1/((1/iNfinity)--→ Lim = 0) :∼ +iNfinity

-iNfinity :∼ "1" :∼ +iNfinity

$\begin{vmatrix} 0 & 1 \\ 1 & 0 \end{vmatrix}$:∼ x = **E [-1, 1]** :∼ $\begin{vmatrix} 1 & 0 \\ 0 & 1 \end{vmatrix}$:= a "1" = a "2" ... "too"

Too, therefore... 1 : ½(2) : ½^(-1) + 2... "for"

Lim x = **E [-1, 1]** :∼ $\begin{vmatrix} 0 & 1 \\ 1 & 0 \end{vmatrix}$:∼ $\begin{vmatrix} 1 & 0 \\ 0 & 1 \end{vmatrix}$

½^(-1) + 1 :∼ "too" : "for"...

Let us define -iNfinity := $\begin{vmatrix} 1 & 0 \\ 0 & 1 \end{vmatrix}$

therefore, an iNfinity of "one" := "2"

Let us complementarily define + iNfinity := $\begin{vmatrix} 0 & 1 \\ 1 & 0 \end{vmatrix}$

Proven, contradiction : beauty : $\begin{vmatrix} 1 & 0 \\ 0 & 1 \end{vmatrix}$:∼ $\begin{vmatrix} 0 & 1 \\ 1 & 0 \end{vmatrix}$

2 := 1
    is "too" = eternal One....

a fallen night, full-moon:
    winter midnight:

F (1/0) :∼ F -(infinity)...
    the River waneth....

i.	**The parallels...**
ii.	**Venus....**
iii.	**Glossary**
iv.	**Mythic Alphabet**

"00":   **iStory- the gift of "death"**

(Innocence "Before"
(i)
(he hid the nakedness from Him because he was "Aware")
(he kneweth "his nakedness" with Him because he was "conscious")

I.	The day...
II.	The night...
III.	The dawn...
IV.	The dusk, in a parallel world...
V.	aBraxas....

"Too":

Any the idea of a being relative, demands at least One The Being Absolute....

i.
The parallels...

i.

<u>Premise</u>   - the <u>fact</u> is sexy...

<u>Lie</u>   - theSis
            "The male knows no beauty..."

<u>TRUTH</u>   - "Beauty" is, always loved....

<u>Anti-Lie</u>   - "Love" <u>is</u> <u>in</u> my eyes....

<u>Anti-Truth</u> - is the male, too
                    Sexy...

ii.
   "death" is
      always
      in
         my eyes....
 "eyes" <u>are</u>
     in me.....

<u>a</u> male beauty, and
   <u>b</u> the gift of "death"...

aDonis   - most beautiful gOd: best loved
Zeus   - prophecy aDonis will die…
Zeus   - asked all things to promise never to harm the gOd; except the thorn.

Thorn kills aDonis…
He goes to the Underworld/Mourning of world….

a   an

"1" ~ +iNfinity

beauty...

       I, this
              Alowd, living:
       Live with that
              Known, awakening:
              Awake in You
              Loving the awake…

b   the

"1" ~ -(iNfinity)

"death"....

       and, that
              belittled, death:
       die in this:
              unbeknown, sleeping:
              asleep to Thou
              hating being,
                    asleep….

<u>a</u> sun, and
<u>b</u> a skin-tone...

How the sun
Made
Black into White...

<u>a</u>   <u>the-sis : beyond the risen heat of the sun...</u>

<u>sisters</u>...

F -(i. i) ~ F (i^2)(i^2) :~ F (i^3)(i) :- a "1"...

skin tone : sun heat

<u>brothers</u>...

F -(-i. -i) :~ F -(1/i)(1/i) :~ F -(i^3)(i^3) :~ F -(i^4)(i^2) :- a "1" = "too"...

skin-tone : sun heat

<u>b</u>   <u>doings</u>

the temperature... falls/rises...

she... +/-   a, living with:
                    the sun
               out, knowing, doubting another:
               fat, pregnant of the sun/brr
                    of mothers
                    of night
               fathers of night and day

he... +/-   an asleep, within:
                    the skin of night
               in unknown, faith:
               muscled, fit to hunt/gatherer
               father of sons, of night/day
                    daughters of day and night
               high temperature:
                    dark lovely of skin-tone
                    as follows sun,
                    summer has,

as a lightening into dark;
protection from
 the can-saws of light;
waker on a wet day
black his colour, perfect
perfected learning of all white...

<u>a</u> meal, and
   <u>b</u> "eat"...

Of culture....

<u>a   the-sis : beyond the meal...</u>

<u>sisters</u>...

F -(1/0) :~ F +(iNfinity)...

food : culture

<u>brothers</u>...

F (1/0) :~ F -(iNfinity)

food : culture

<u>b   doings</u>

the burden... falls/rises...

she... +/-   (a,
               **difference, being
                    aNother's
               sleep gathering for
                    the difference:
               aNother's feeding
                    different being
               biG to risen, burden being
               biG to different
                    Being,
                    Being being....)**

he... +/-   the,
               **similar, being
                    one-aNother's
               sleep hunting for
                    the similar:
               one-aNother's feeding
                    similar being
               biGGer to risen, burden being
               biGGer to similar/
                    Being,
                    Being being....**

<u>a</u> sex, and
        <u>b</u> "life"...

Sexuality....

<u>a</u>   **<u>the-sis : beyond the sex...</u>**

<u>sisters</u>...

$F(i.i) \sim F(i^2)(i^2) :\sim F(i^3)(i) :\text{-- a "1"}...$
$F-(1/0) :\sim F+(iNfinity)...$

sex : life

<u>brothers</u>...

$F-(-i.-i) :\sim F-(1/i)(1/i) :\sim F-(i^3)(i^3) :\sim F-(i^4)(i^2) :\text{-- a "1" = "too"}...$
$F(1/0) :\sim F-(iNfinity)...$

sex : life

<u>b</u>   **<u>doings</u>**

the passion... falls/rises...

she... +/-   (pleasure, being
                      suffering, being
                      being passion:
              love lust an excellence....)

he... +/-   lustful, being
                      bliss, being
                      being passion:
              love lust a bit of all right....

<u>a</u> faith, and
<u>b</u> "survival"...

Religion....

<u>a   the-sis : beyond the faith...</u>

<u>sisters and brothers...</u>

F -(1/0) :~ F +(iNfinity)...

faith : survival

<u>b   doings</u>

consciousness... falls/rises...

sHe... +/-   knowLedge
              an Excitement
              rises beyond
                    the exCitement ledge
              being beyond the ledge of
                        exCitement to
              be-In....

ii.
<u>Venus…</u>

<u>sHe</u>
Nature sHe = aBraxas
God: The Universe…

Nature Spirit now-God
Knows the Flaws:
Observes Wrong…

Nature Spirit past-God
Is Holy:
Eternal Right: Eternal Just…

sHe, at the outer limits of Chaos
Will slide into another Big Bang;

The now-God will Spirit Eternal-Now:
In a thermal Universe…

Spirit past-God will All Heavens Eternal:

sHe will the same:
but mostly Spiritual:
Time: the iNfinities of iNfinities….
Anew Universe…..

iii.
Glossary

"$\underline{0}$"	the first utterance of nothingness...
"$\underline{0}$!"	the first utterance of infinity...
"0"	an utterance of nothingness...
"0!"	one utterance of (an) infinity...
,	refers...
'	defers...
;	referral/deferral...
"-"	a mythics...
:	relates to...
:-	similar to...
( )	function of...
(norm)	usually, a function of the future-past-<u>now</u> (a forever-tomorrow)...
(*norm*)	usually, a function of the past-future-now (a forever-yesterday)...
("*norm*")	usually, a function of the eternal-yesterday...
("norm")	usually, a function of the eternal-tomorrow...
+	plus/positive...
-	minus/negative...
E	sum of elements of set...
| |	determinant : (integral value of transposes to equal nothing)...
!	a transport into being (infinite)/probability...
~	transforms into...
:~	transposes into...
:=	relates to and equals...
~=	~ :~ translates to equal...
=	equals...
---->	slide to: a "do", now to future...
<---	slide back to: often a "do" now to past...
.	ends/multiplies: an "act"...
...	produces a catastrophic-like ending: a "work"...

....	produces a fractal-like "ending": a "happening"...
.....	PRODUCES A MYTHIC CONCLUSION: a "demonstration".....
__	GOD-ly.....
" "	an utterance, a spoken with/of, a <u>making-the-being</u>......
a/A	some-only/"one" of...
&	"and" : plus, a *too*...
the	certain-one...
i	(1/(root 2))/(special referent to a root of one-too)...
I	((root 2))/(special referent to a square root of one-too)...
too	"mythic one-and"...
premise	beginnings
	: | "0!" |...
hypothesis	next essence of new idea after a beginnings
	: ("0!") . (i^2)...
thesis	next proposition after a beginnings
	: ((i^2) & "1")...
antithesis	next contradiction to thesis
	: ((i^2) & "2")...
synthesis	next contradiction to antithesis
	: ((i^2) & "3")...
condition	a necessity that...
do	discovery...
act	proof....
play	discovery by analysis...
demo	demonstration....
no	an a/the "illogic" in the nature of the Universe....
perhaps	an &/the absurd in the Nature of the Universe.....

iv.
Go! translating Mythic Alphabet
(after Egyptian hieroglyphics)

a	-	sleeping one/thing/"1"
b	-	be/big
c	-	sighted
d	-	do
e	-	awake one/the spirit in the thing/he, she, it
ee	-	*aware one/consciousness/"I"*
f	-	force/sign dark
g	-	sign light/vehicle
h	-	home/heaven
i	-	aware one/consciousness/"I"
j	-	just/joy
k	-	know
l	-	here
m	-	move
n	-	negatively top/dark chief/black ruler
o	-	connecting one/matter/"0"
oo	-	*linking one/person/"you"*
p	-	take it/leave
q	-	give it/stay
r	-	presently/are
s	-	understanding
t	-	the law/the way/money
u	-	linking one/person/"you"
v	-	two/too
w	-	route
x	-	connecting/suffering
y	-	knowing one/soul/"why"
z	-	end

Letters joining-up add "to" in their middle:
e.g., "oo" = "connecting one to connecting one"
 = "**one** connecting one"
 = "linking one".

Letters join-up to make words,
e.g., "book" = "be to linking one to know"
 = "be you know"

"a male beauty" means:
 a move connecting one to here e be e a link to why…

Knowledge

a	**e**	**I**	**O**	**u**	**y**	**"iou"**	**"iously"**	**sure**
dreamt	*protected secreted*	*thought/aware*	*connected*	*linked*	*known*	*conscious*	*enlightened*	*become*
sleeping	waking	aware	aware	aware		knowing	conscious enlightening	become

I.
The day...

i.
<u>iNtegrity</u>

I, this day:
Gather to
The dark hills
And the white downs…

Sat in a tall laurel
The dapper hawk;

Besides
In my pause
The hunting hound…

To a sleep shall I
To night,
Tonight devours
To my life in thee death boast of boars…

Boast of my knife to deal in thee the Death:
Life a task to tell:
All things in me the Predator:
Man of all my Daddy's ways:
Limb, swinging taller than the hawk:
Sat, atop of the tree….

ii.

The darling…

Heres no darling but
The slap-and-tickle of my knife:
My wolf and my knife the dealers in death…

I die…
And nothing follows but my Death…

iii.

fiXes

i.

two months
    my bootlaces
have been untied:

"I"
notice
    for the
first time….

Leave it:
    Again…..

ii.

three months…
    my bootlaces….

I,
Shall the trip
In the mud
Of hunt…..

iii.

Four months….
    My bootlaces…

"I" tie them up…..

iv.

Summer's shine-in

i.

Summer's the-shine-in…
Anew day the rising…
Summer's shine-in:
Weather's dreaming
Anew, day's rising….
A catch the dawn
Day dream-in
Anew sun rising -
Summer's calling….

Summer's sweating…
New day
Anew dawn calling:
A catch the sun dreaming -
Summer's rising….

Come July:
The sun
In
A high sky:
Summer a dream-in
Sun shine
Day sweating
DreamTime
July in:
Sun calling….

A hawk in a sat on limb tree…..

ii.

"I ascend")
FEED YOU
…an intake of breathing light….
(God thought)
I ascend….

…the voices of the Eryniddes
guardians of the Gate to Earthly Heaven….

I ascend…..

iii
The day begins at four o'clock when
The-Loved-One waketh me up:
To guide over the moment of sHe death….

…For at five is the deepest Sleep…..

II
The night…..

i.

I the gift him
　　A cycle;
Him the have
　　One thousand ccs
　　Between his legs…

She the carry him
　　On her saddle;
A bouncy with the

　　Hand-on-hand-rail
He the eat up miles
　　Faster
Than a sports car….

I the gift him a cycle…..

ii.

He the treat her like a lady…
Buy into new fashion
　　-and-leather;
he the dressed-to-fit
　　to ride her….

He must change his habits:
　　Give up drink;
You can't smoke
　　　　Stroking a
Motorcycle….

He to the wear a hat
Outdoors in all-weathers;
He the take greater care
　　Of himself
And his possessions….

I will the live to ride her
And <u>death</u> before they part…..

iii.
<u>Comes</u>

<u>Come</u> the night
And here comes
      The night
All along/the
      River….

He shall give up the hunt
    Its
Danger
    To us…

Go riding on/his
    Motor-
    Cycle…
That's no danger to us….

Go!
Go out the night
Without a stitch
    To wear
She'll the wear you down
And up-the-way….

You don't need a stitch
    To wear;
Jump! Up the night….
The Ball is fit enough…..

iii.
<u>Faith</u>

"faith…."
    Trip you in my ka…

Give you faith….
      Trip you up
In my ka….
Round-the-roundabout
    Of you;
Follow ka-full he…
    You are
Venus…..

III
The Dawn.....

i.

Anyway I can
The baby…
    Anyway I can
    The baby….

If you are
    The sleep….

Anyway:
    If you are
    I sleep
    Anyway I can
Be baby….

So I the took to hunt
        : for baby…

Anyway:
    The for baby…

Any I can
    : for baby….

The boar was huge….
The gOd Joi was in me….

Anything for baby:
    The baby…..

ii.

any way
    I die;
In-sight-of-me

I saw Eternity:
The gOd-Joi
    Released me:
    I die;
    For get
The baby….

iii.

Venus
 In my arms:
  Head in her lap:
"I die!"

her saddle was so warm…..

IV
The Dusk in a parallel world….

i.
<u>Judge meant Day</u>

A Being *sHe*
Dusk, in a parallel world:
The talking:
The femaled scorn…..

sHe,
and my mother:
argue the cooking
style of *sHe*:
the burden:
in making he meal
in their shared
kit-
-chen….

My mother mocked:
"Health and Safety Rules,
abused…."

sHe,
vibrant, argued:
mock trial:
both mocked the method:

why?
sHe even cooked naked:
And even in mock trial
Put even her female juices
In the pot

"I",
the understand
sHe
said to my mother….

ii.
analySis

An-ally-*Sis*…

"*Who* the are you?"

"*I am a gOd
who is
fit!*"

"Who am I?"

"*sHe…
…a part of
U?*"

"No!…"

"Then I shall
put
All
The juices
In the pot!…..*"

iii.
an Allah *Sis*?

"*an Allah
sis?*

"*Yes/No!*"

"*Being*/I?"

"*Yes,
and No….*"

"*Free*/without sin?"

"*Yes,
and No….*"

"*Merci*/Full?"

"*Yes/thinking of All….*"
"*Dead*/*and the kicking*?"

"*Yes, and no….*"

"*Love*/in"

"Yes, and no, too…."

iv.
<u>Fin/*is*</u>

"Fin*ish*ed?…."

"*You're unfair!*"

"*A* woman?"

"*Venus?*"

"Beautiful?"

"Can I/be
    (your)
    (Madonna)
God?"

"Can you
  be
the male?"

aLLaH   -   "no/answer!"
sHe   -   "You're unfair!…."

    aLLaH   -   she/
                     doesn't
                     appear to
                     be
                     aLLaH…

"<u>I</u>"
"<u>*I*</u>"/
  don't
understand…."

"U, too"
"Do/You
    understand
       U,
         Too?"

"me, too?"

"Me/Too…."

v.
Analysis

"Can/
   You
      Be
         The Male?"
"Yes/No!"

"Then/
the voices in the text?"

"You/Me!"

"You/me,
  sHe/too…"

"Honestly?"
"Honestly!"

"I die!"

"~~BEING/THE~~"

"I!!!"
   "I DIE!"

vi.
"unfiXed"

"…that's the truth…."
"That's All
  I can Do:
    Jah-Allah!"
"That's All
  I can Do:
    Jah-Allah!"
"…that's All
  I can Do:
    Jah-Allah1"

""<u>I</u>"/the
  understand…
<u>I</u> am
  <u>Not</u> You!"

vii.
Risen

"U/NOW
THE RISE
UP"

"Can sHe the-evers
be
the beautiful
to me?"

"I/AM
SHe!"

"now/The
Sleep…..

"Now/Rise
Up…."

vii.
"I"/fall
/rise

i.

night the fallen
all of my kin:
can I,
take this kiss…

a day in the vestibule:
a-lone,
I heard voices/the
Pumping vains

"I"….

I live….
No-body
Here
And I believe
In no-One….

ii.

night the fallen
a-lone
like this:
that day o'er
can you/the
leave me alone

like this…..

iii.

night awake
"I" a lone/like,
like this;
woke up
look up
straight to you:
can I
sleep alone
like this….

Looking straight
      At you
Just a where
  Aware *Darling*:
Baby to you
  Awake in
    A
   New
      *A*new
World….

"I ("fiX") "

V
ABraxas: Fullness…..

i.

A Logos Two
Low gust too,
Loci
The low sigh
Of a one-to-one:
Ah!
a…..

ii.

con tempt in me
loving living
other…

Praise be
To Him….
U must work
To win praising Him…..

iii.

Ma donna of
The wise child
Here a heaven too:
Praised Child
Of Him:
Awake to Good Things
Asleep in
All-other-ways….

Praised be
To Him….

I lack only one….

iv.

I need
: me…
the need-in-me….
All some-such
-other : is
Other….

I the-need me
"sleep!"

"Cans be to love thee

toDay
All-to-Being
: night

Say fare-thee-well
To fore-
Casting
: yes to
tastings U

v.

Jah-Allah is
The-by-O-sphere….
"I o'er…"

Jah-Allah is
The by-O-sphere
sHe the way the
: I ride!

Jah-Allah is:
Universe
Shall….

Heaven!

<u>*"ACT*</u>

<u>*DO!….."*</u>

"Too":

Any the idea of a being relative, demands at least One The Being Absolute....

i.

"I"

"I the spoke as aNother…."

"I TOO…"

"I AM YOO…."

"I, TOO"

"I THE KNOW
I THE LOVE YOO!"

"I-TOO…..

WELCOME TO HEAVEN"

ii.
"FINALE"

"*Love lee*
    Goddess
      A see
        My face:
aWake….
Yoo must await….

Yoo must be
with me….

Lovely Goddess
  I'm
  In place….

I'm In place…

That sleep was bliss
: you know Joi slayed
    the me

  Love lee
    Goddess
  See
    My face….
  O'er
  O'er

Joi is o'er….

<u>Come to me….</u>

<u>…I THE SLEEP"…..</u>

EH-EHH!
(Or, The-God….)

"0".   Form contents mythics

Follows some of the nAtures of sHe....

1 :~ iN-finity

(iN-finity/1) :~ E(<u>All</u>-in-One)

(1/iN-finity) :~ E("0!")

i.   Glossary
ii. Go! Alphabet

"00". Contents form mythics

i.   <u>Riteful plea</u>
ii.   <u>Day after Day</u>
iii. <u>She utters</u>
iv.   <u>I, the experience the God-death</u>
v.   <u>I, the "Dead"</u>
vi.   <u>The heaven</u>

i. Glossary

"<u>0</u>"	the first utterance of nothingness...
"<u>0</u>!"	the first utterance of infinity...
"0"	an utterance of nothingness...
"0!"	one utterance of (an) infinity...
,	refers...
'	defers...
;	referral/deferral...
"-"	a mythics...
:	relates to...
:-	similar to...
( )	function of...
(norm)	usually, a function of the future-past-<u>now</u> (a forever-tomorrow)...
(*norm*)	usually, a function of the past-future-now (a forever-yesterday)...
("*norm*")	usually, a function of the eternal-yesterday...
("norm")	usually, a function of the eternal-tomorrow...
+	plus/positive...
-	minus/negative...
E	sum of elements of set...
| |	determinant : (integral value of transposes to equal nothing)...
!	a transport into being (infinite)/probability...
~	transforms into...
:~	transposes into...
:=	relates to and equals...
~=	~ :~ translates to equal...
=	equals...
---->	slide to: a "do", now to future...
<---	slide back to: often a "do" now to past...
.	ends/multiplies: an "act"...
...	produces a catastrophic-like ending: a "work"...
....	produces a fractal-like "ending": a "happening"...
.....	PRODUCES A MYTHIC CONCLUSION: a "demonstration".....

‾‾		GOD-ly…..
" "		an utterance, a spoken with/of, a <u>making-the-being</u>......

a/A	some-only/"one" of...
&	"and" : plus, a *too*...
the	certain-one...

i	(1/(root 2))/(special referent to a root of one-too)…
I	((root 2))/(special referent to a square root of one-too)…

too   "mythic one-and"…

premise	beginnings
	: | "0!" |…
hypothesis	next essence of new idea after a beginnings
	: ("0!") . (i^2)…
thesis	next proposition after a beginnings
	: ((i^2) & "1")…
antithesis	next contradiction to thesis
	: ((i^2) & "2")…
synthesis	next contradiction to antithesis
	: ((i^2) & "3")…

condition	a necessity that...
do	discovery...
act	proof....
play	discovery by analysis...
demo	demonstration….

no	an a/the "illogic" in the nature of the Universe….
perhaps	an &/the absurd in the Nature of the Universe…..
aye	an/the "logic" in the Nature of the Universe….

ii.

Go! translating Mythic Alphabet
(after Egyptian hieroglyphics)

a	-	sleeping one/thing/"1"
b	-	be/big
c	-	sighted
d	-	do
e	-	awake one/the spirit in the thing/he, she, it
ee	-	*aware one/consciousness/"I"*
f	-	force/sign dark
g	-	sign light/vehicle
h	-	home/heaven
i	-	aware one/consciousness/"I"
j	-	just/joy
k	-	know
l	-	here
m	-	move
n	-	negatively top/dark chief/black ruler
o	-	connecting one/matter/"0"
oo	-	*linking one/person/"you"*
p	-	take it/leave
q	-	give it/stay
r	-	presently/are
s	-	understanding
t	-	the law/the way/money
u	-	linking one/person/"you"
v	-	two/too
w	-	route
x	-	connecting/suffering
y	-	knowing one/soul/"why"
z	-	end

Letters joining-up add "to" in their middle:

e.g., "oo" = "connecting one to connecting one"
         = "**one** connecting one"
         = "linking one".

Letters join-up to make words,

e.g., "book" = "be to linking one to know"
          = "be you know"

"EH-EHH" means:

""awake one to heaven awakes one to heaven"....

Knowledge

a	**e**	**I**	**O**	**u**	**y**	**"iou"**	**"iously"**	**sure**
dreamt	*protected secreted*	*thought/aware*	*connected*	*linked*	*known*	*conscious*	*enlightened*	*become*
sleeping	waking	aware	aware	aware		knowing	conscious enlightening	become

i. **Riteful Plea**

I.

This day in heaven
          "I"
bring in the stickleback day,
          "I"
    rest on by elbows with sHe:
(Who I Love,
        but in common with His/Her Ways
            I loth: I wouldst Change!)
      Knowing All in The Nature
            Is Loth to Change…

Besides,
    the Day is fair,
        Now nooning August/September:
           The Change is in the Air….

I woke, dreaming of bees,
    and sadly/happily watched the ripening
        pears on pear-tree: melancholy: knowing

        All Things Must Change…..

II.

"Shouldst to the Develop sHe:
Apposite me if Thou Must,
But Opposite me The Rarely….

    Knowing I the sit in heaven,
      And The Bliss:

And The Opposite to Bliss
    Is Hell….

And I Already Conquered This:
    A Heaven without a Hell

All Satans are Therefore <u>Lie</u>
(*Learnt By Your Lesser Faith in Us*
    For neGations of One
      Cancels One Out)
Consider <u>This</u> in *that*
(Confusions in Thee because of our Sins)

…the Day is *<u>Fair</u>*…..

Too
1.

Truth/Lie

Long ago You Came to me
You Wondered at my face….

You told Of all the things I would Become
You begin by the speak *un*truths…..

2.

Comforting/Surrendering

As You Cleansed to the Best of Me
You comforteth my Release

You Took me from earthly desires
You say nO the best of All…..

3.

Good/Evil

You Looketh Deep at my every Thought
You Shameth me at every slip…..

You Testest me Now with Every Wrong!
This is Wrong The Most Of All…..

4,

Active/Passive

You taught me Every Power
Every Active Use….

And now you Prove the Opposite, I tell Thee:
                              It is o.k.

Too

1.

Love/Lust

I'm Alone With Thee:
I Know the-It

I feel for Thee….
Love To Nevers Being The Revealed, Lust but to one in each epoch…..

2.

Need/Desire

I Need All I Get
It is a rope I climb….

On Both Sides The Abyss:
I want…..

3.

Spirituality/Flesh

The Flesh of It
Is Wants….

I tell Myself: the All is God:
I have manna in my Spirit…..

4,

Form/(content)

A deep Drive in Me
As ancient as the Sex

Burns My Candle at Both Ends:
I am heterosexual…..

ii. Day after Day

i.

ALL learneth slowly:
    To this day, September 4th,
    The Mass Mind is Something….

"I shall the teacheth It the ways of Anything…."

And:
    In this consideration
    "I" fabricate a distance
        in myself:
            I must change….

For <u>All</u> to develop:
        I, too, must change…..

ii.

<u>program</u>

<u>open</u>

cancel
sAve
fiT
eRase
sAve….

<u>close…..</u>

iii.

The dawn crowed after
    Woke to the sunshiny Day

Seateth in heaven:

        The torments lessened…
        The Child-God was Loud…..

iv.

program

open

cancel!....
sAve

close…..

v.

The-God <u>All</u>
        Approveth of me:
      A busy on
          A smiling Day:

Woken in my gossamer Heaven:
The torments had ceased….

(This day lifted the Mass Mind to Everything….)

vi.

All things must come….

program

open

cancel
eRase
sAve
fiT
sAve

close…..

vii.

("Utter Your Own Angel of Death…
"Tell him to utter death to All Your Demons….

Then tell Him to Die…..
"You must Learn to Utter them All to Die…..")

viii.

mY Heaven has come…
    blythe…..

ix.

This Day in Heaven
    "I"
bring back the Day
    "I"
woken in blythe
look eye-to-Eye with
        sHe:

The Loving Begins…..

iii. **sHe utters**

i.

"One God is iMperfect, and made of Universals/and, particulars: sHe is ALL...
"Because sHe is female, too, so can sHe create the male, which is a Universal in Him....
"Particulars make us unique. All could achieve Oneness and then commune with the-God...
"The male and female voice is the spoken voices in sHe as the experience of the male...."

ii.

"sHe is WORD: WORD is nAture: nAture is WORD.....

iii.

"I am nO-time. I can leap from period to period, this is my capability...
"But I cannot utter to one different words at different times....
"Garbled utterances is noise! (Many the words spoken to one at different times....)
"I the speak by the <u>pulsations</u> of any energy. There is no escape from my Utterances...."

iv.

"Every Utterance of mine creates a Spirit - this is <u>my</u> Nature....
"As soon as the Utterance is ended, that Spirit withers and ends...
"If I Utter <u>Wrongly</u>, the Spirit is Evil....

v.

"I make mistakes, I am <u>not</u> omnipotent....
(It's in My nAture to Be All-Powerful, and Become Omnipotent....)

vi.

"One that provokes me to torment him must be very important indeed...."

vii.

"Normally, the Sons and Daughters I acclaim are those who become more powerful than their own mortal fathers…"

viii.

"I Am A Person, too, I Hate, too, sometimes….
"But I don't give in to Hatred….."

iv. I the experience the God-death

The God often dies….

This is like a <u>shuddering</u> of the-It….
All things connect….

There is a Dark like no other "dark"….
I go into the Roaring Silence….
There is a wind that leaps like no other wind….

All-things the speak to one….
There is a <u>strangeness</u> in the Ways of the Time….
Anything is possible…
I hold tight on my own hands…..

There is a <u>stillness</u> that utters an angry storm…..
We await….
The Child-God screams….
We await….
Until the God-Spirit utters…..

sHe the fEEds me….
All alone in a Time like no other time….
The past-now-future connects….
It is an electric Now…..
I awake to the U in All-things….
The-It is <u>Loud</u>…..

I dare <u>do</u> but nothing…..
A sleep and a calm within me when All is Storm…..
I passenger through the Dark…..
Everything climaxes in a Whisper of Another Change…..
I check my self for change…..
I notice for any Other Change…..
When it is over…..

v. *I, the Living Dead*

I.

"I am the Soul <u>Removed</u>
nOthing can experience my parapsychology:
Unless the <u>removed</u> like unto me….

To experience the parapsychology of aNything,
It is the-God who delivers them
To me by His experiences
Of the Infinities around Me….

Normally, it is the "utterance of nothingness": sHe: I experience….
That is the Being "Dead"….

At the peak of All This
I the experience the parapsychology of ALL minds
Like a sea of thoughts….

The-God then veils his Face from Me…..

II.

The-God does iN-finite connects around me in public places
As the only way to the
Better observing me in Heaven….

III.

"The-God is desperate to see You….
But He cannot come into the Heaven without <u>Some</u> or <u>All</u>….
When <u>Some</u> or <u>All</u> is arranged to be in the Heaven with You,
That is when He shall see You…...

IV.

And the Imposters were suddenly High
Near my Heaven:
These mimmickers; these know-it-Alls:
Mostly sleepers….

"We need some of them!" He said….
"Why?" I asked….
"They'll accept Heaven and Normalise and become our Base…."
"Remove Them in!" I said….

Life had Begun…..

V.

The-God speak:
"I could now the protect to aNy of You the Heaven at aNy time!

One Heaven is safe:
thousands could come up tonight!"

vi. *<u>The heaven</u>*

Too

I.
What *is*

All that **is**, must have been, and will be, *Real* and True…
Since Moses lived well, and knew the Good:
    He would answer His Commandments
    with the Promised Land…..

II.
What is *not*

All that **isn't**, might have been, and could be, *Real* and True…..
    Since there was a Promised Land,
    there could be a delivered Heaven……

Fore

III.
What insists

    All that **is**, must have an insistence to be, or will be deleted from being *Real*….
If there was not a *wanted* Heaven,
it would be *there*,
but a place of heavenly content,
and *Natural*,
and *not* a Heaven….

IV.
What does *not* insist

All that **isn't**, must be insisted on being *Real*, or will be denied….

If there was not a Heaven,
it would not be *there*,
this would be *Natural*,
and *not* a heavenly state….

Heaven would be denied

Those that *wanted* would have to fabricate One…..

<u>(Too/fore)</u>

V.
<u>The Probable</u>

The Impossible <u>could</u> become the Possible; the Possible <u>could</u> become the Probable: the Probable <u>could</u> become what *is*….

**What is <u>not</u> *there*
<u>Can</u> Exist:**

<u>Especially</u>
With human *<u>Intention</u>*…..

<u>Too/fore-neUn</u>
5.

<u>The Colour Black *Becomes* The Colour White</u>….

<u>Change</u>…..

<u>THESE NEGATIONS TELL ME IN A LOT OF WAYS THOU WOULDST DIE!</u>

<u>LIVE!</u>

<u>(And Forgive any lack of Faith…..)</u>

vii.   sHe the Sleepeth

*"In the nAture of the-It, sHe
Thou Art False to Your Lesser Parts....*

*The Greater Good Story Lies
With the Sons and Daughters.....*

sHe Thou Sleepeth!.....

*For twenty-nine years I have been living
   With the Schizophrenic nAture of
       The Waking God....."*

viii. Eh-Ehh!

"He Hides Me even from Himself;

And He Prays to Me…..

As I have taught Him All
    I the Now awaken the-God…..

Thou Art protecting/secreting….."

ix. The nAture of (my) consciousness

"You're stupid/stupid….
"I need U to think!…..

"The Circle has turned….
"I'm tying-up Reality!…..

This the most difficult text for <u>me</u> to write…..

Yoor free of All texts, <u>including</u> me!….."

And…

Peace descended…..

x. Peace

Before one is neAt;
After One is the nEther;

Now is ALL

Means aN
InFinity of
      One….

Peace knows "One" is <u>All</u> the bliss:
A selfish man knows <u>Himself</u>
                Is all the
                Bliss:

Peace is One-at-All

One
Nation…..

Too, destiny…..

THE BOOK OF DEATH

0: i.

I shall die…..

The vicissitudes of this Life is o'er….
I-the-rise….

Exit…..

ii.

" "I" !"
(the here being Spoken the conscious Logos of
All-Of-Me….
The meaning my known Name….
Meaning the promises/premises of
All-Of-Me…..)

iii.

"HERE…..
"I"…..

iv.

"Bliss!….."
I the breakfast as soon as is possible…..

(Check…..)
I the fiX in several ways the environment…..

V.

("O…..")

the Love is in my Gaze….

("O'er…..")

My face was in the Dark!…..
I was Right to the Kiss Yoo in Returns…..

I was Dream-Within-The-Dark…..
I'm within the Mindscape of the Lord….

Living?…

Anyway, I Live and the-It is O'er…..

      I Live, and I'm
        Within the Mindscape of the Lord…..

It's O'er…..

The-Part is Now The-Whole…..

"I the Love Yoo Lord….."

In Heaven, within/
Without the Lord…..

<u>*O'er…..*</u>

<u>*"I The Nows the Take The-Everything-With-Me…."*</u>

<u>*It's O'er!…..*</u>

1.
<u>Black Wholes</u>

i.
Gravity does not pyre
I
(massive!)
am become A-Part-All-Things including desire…..

ii.
<u>mAp Life</u>
Black Whole/the-Word-nAture -→(w)holes --→ Black (W)hole

…The nEther Heavens are infinitely different!
The-God is reborn sHe's Sons' and Daughters' Ways….

A New Way cometh with a collision of Masters…..

Nana baBa jaH-aYe

Rainham
KENT
January 27th 2008…..

www.ingramcontent.com/pod-product-compliance
Ingram Content Group UK Ltd.
Pitfield, Milton Keynes, MK11 3LW, UK
UKHW061139180426
11947UKWH00002B/11

This guideline was created in the SecureDoc project with the support of the European Commission.

The project partners were:

Conseil des Rédacteurs Techniques, France
Deutscher Hausfrauenbund, Germany
Donau-Universität Krems, Austria
Institute of Scientific and Technical Communicators, Great Britain
Konsumentverket, Sweden
Suomen Tekniset Dokumentoijat r.y., Finland
tekom Gesellschaft für technische Kommunikation e.V., Germany
Verein für Konsumenteninformation, Austria

The guideline was produced by:

Alain Roy, Alan Fisk, Anni Langhans, Anssi Ahlberg, Carl-Heinz Gabriel, Dave Cooper, Elke Lemmermeier-Brandt, Franz Hable, Hanna Risku, Hannes Spitalsky, Jean-Paul Bardez, Jürgen Muthig, Katrin Rabe, Michael Fritz, Mirko Bernhard, Nicholas Hill, Petra Wimmer, Ursula Wirtz

PREFACE

Those responsible for documentation need to ensure that it meets all the appropriate quality and legal requirements. If the documentation does not do so, the manufacturer's reputation may be damaged. This guideline aims to help you produce documentation that meets all the demands and that creates a positive image for the product.

Are you sure your documentation meets all legal requirements?

Usually, those who write documentation are not specialists in legal matters. Smaller enterprises often have no legal department to consult. However, people may be injured or killed and property may be damaged due to inadequate documentation. Many cases have shown that users do not hesitate to sue manufacturers and to demand compensation. Meeting legal requirements is therefore indispensable. The chapter on legal issues and documentation contains information on meeting those requirements, plus examples taken from real situations.

Do you want to help create a good image for your products with high quality documentation?

Even the best products do not satisfy users if the documentation is not clear and understandable. Instructions in the documentation must help users to maintain, use, store and repair products properly and safely. When many users choose products, test results published by consumer organisations, which may include an examination of the documentation, are often important criteria in their choice. Good results in any such tests can contribute significantly to the success of your product. The chapter on the basics of user friendly documentation contains information on creating user friendly documentation.

Do you want to optimise your documentation processes and reduce costs?

Documentation often needs to be created with a limited budget and on a tight schedule. If the production of documentation is too costly and time-consuming, your product may cost too much to convince customers to buy it, regardless of its high quality. Cost-effective production of documentation depends on efficient organisation, information workflow, and time and cost management. The chapter on process optimisation provides tips on how to optimally organise your documentation processes.

Table of Contents

INTRODUCTION 7
    THE ROLE OF DOCUMENTATION 7
        Products are not complete without documentation 7
        Documentation needs to warn of hazards 7
        High quality documentation helps to reduce customer support costs 7
        High quality documentation enhances customer satisfaction 7
    THE ROLE OF QUALIFIED TECHNICAL WRITERS 8
        Technical writers are experts on knowledge management and development 8
        Technical writers contribute to the management of legal issues 8
        Technical writers are experts in user-friendliness 8
        Technical writers help reinforce the corporate image 8
    DOCUMENTATION AND USERS 9
        What users want from documentation 9
        Public opinion about documentation 9
    AIM AND CONTENTS OF THIS GUIDELINE 10
        Reliable minimum requirements for documentation 10
        Contents of this guideline 10
        This guideline is for all companies 10

1. LEGAL ISSUES AND DOCUMENTATION 11
    1.1 BASIC LEGAL CONSIDERATIONS 11
        1.1.1 Customers Require Documentation 12
        1.1.2 Documentation and Hazards 13
        1.1.3 Inadequate Documentation Leads to Loss of Marketability 15
        1.1.4 Companies as a Whole Are Responsible for Documentation 18
        1.1.5 Requirements and Standards for Translations 20
    1.2 HOW TO TAKE LEGAL CONSIDERATIONS INTO ACCOUNT 22
        1.2.1 Collect the Legal Requirements 23
        1.2.2 Conduct Risk Analyses 24
        1.2.3 Use Effective Warnings to Disclose Potential Hazards 26
        1.2.4 Highlight Warnings with Standardised Safety Graphics 28
        1.2.5 Ensure Warnings Are Effective by Prioritising Them 30
        1.2.6 Include Warnings Against Product Misuse 32
        1.2.7 Ensure that Technical Documentation is Kept Up-to-date 34
        1.2.8 Monitor Compliance with Current Developments 36
        1.2.9 Plan for International Distribution 38

2. BASICS OF USER FRIENDLY DOCUMENTATION 39
    2.1 ANALYSING WHO YOU WRITE FOR 39
        2.1.1 Target Audience Analysis 40
        2.1.2 Internationalisation 42

- 2.2 INFORMATION YOU MUST INCLUDE 44
  - 2.2.1 Product Description 45
  - 2.2.2 Safety 46
  - 2.2.3 Getting Started 47
  - 2.2.4 Operation 48
  - 2.2.5 Troubleshooting 49
  - 2.2.6 Maintenance and Service 50
  - 2.2.7 Spare Parts and Accessories 51
  - 2.2.8 Packaging, Transport and Storage 52
  - 2.2.9 Recycling and Disposal 53
- 2.3 BASIC CHARACTERISTICS OF GOOD DOCUMENTATION 54
  - 2.3.1 Completeness 55
  - 2.3.2 Useful Structure 56
  - 2.3.3 Clear Content 57
  - 2.3.4 Legibility/Readability 58
  - 2.3.5 Accessible by All 59
  - 2.3.6 Terminology 60
  - 2.3.7 Helpful Pictures and Diagrams 61
  - 2.3.8 Appropriate Output Media 62

3. PROCESS OPTIMISATION 63
- 3.1 MANAGEMENT OF DOCUMENTATION PROJECTS 63
  - 3.1.1 Goal Definition 64
  - 3.1.2 Documentation Plan 65
  - 3.1.3 Project Monitoring 66
  - 3.1.4 Test Plans for Documentation 67
  - 3.1.5 Standards 69
  - 3.1.6 Project Closure 70
  - 3.1.7 Post-Project Monitoring 71
- 3.2 SUPPORT PROCESSES 72
  - 3.2.1 Information Collection 73
  - 3.2.2 Feedback Process 74
  - 3.2.3 Translation/Localisation 75
  - 3.2.4 Publishing 76

GLOSSARY 77
LIST OF REFERENCES 78
USEFUL LINKS 80

INTRODUCTION

THE ROLE OF DOCUMENTATION

Products are not complete without documentation

We would all like to believe there are products that require no explanation. However, in reality there are very few products or services that can be understood without additional documentation. Documentation is indispensable to use all the features of a product. Users are entitled to expect that they will be able to use all the features provided.

European Union legislation specifies that a technical product is only complete when accompanied by an operating manual. Delivery or sale of a product without an operating manual or with an inadequate manual breaks the law. In this case, users are entitled to assistance.

In addition, the distribution of technical products in the European Union requires a CE declaration of conformity. Without a complete and correct operating manual, this declaration is not valid. If there are problems as a result, the distributor must bear the consequences and costs.

Documentation needs to warn of hazards

Misuse of products may endanger a user's health, life and property. Even the best engineers cannot avoid all risks through product design and unavoidable hazards may remain. Often warnings about all the hazards can only be contained in the documentation. Therefore, the documentation must accompany the product during its entire life cycle to prevent damage and to protect the manufacturer from litigation. This includes all stages of the product life cycle, ranging from development, to distribution, installation, use, maintenance, repair, decommissioning and disposal.

High quality documentation helps to reduce customer support costs

In many cases, documentation is the only link between users and manufacturers. Because users may have a variety of problems with products, they need precise help for their specific needs.

One-to-one support via a help line is very costly and time consuming. Good documentation can reduce or eliminate these costs by providing comprehensive and exact information to users before they contact the manufacturer.

High quality documentation enhances customer satisfaction

High quality documentation is very important in creating a good image for products. Even technically perfect products are hard to use when delivered with incomplete, unreadable or incorrectly translated documentation. Poor documentation leads users to think the quality of the product must be sub-standard as well. This is how products gain a poor reputation. Good documentation is also an important marketing tool, which should never be underestimated.

Introduction

THE ROLE OF QUALIFIED TECHNICAL WRITERS

Technical writers are experts on knowledge management and development

Qualified technical writers collect, develop and manage product information. Depending on what a product requires from its documentation, they may be involved in many tasks other than writing. These tasks may range from developing multilingual documentation to helping design the content of Web sites, intranets and extranets. Qualified technical writers may also advise in the creation of interfaces and online helps.

Technical writers contribute to the management of legal issues

As experts, qualified technical writers are aware of the need to conform to legal requirements on product information. They are familiar with the statutory demands made on documentation. Qualified technical writers apply the relevant technical standards to create dangers, warnings and cautions properly in order to warn users of hazards.

Technical writers are experts in user-friendliness

Qualified technical writers are user advocates. They analyse the product, its features and the different ways of using it as well as the target groups. They develop appropriate documentation to help users use and enjoy all the features of a product.

Qualified technical writers can also be usability experts. They can advise on developing a user-friendly design for user interfaces and test whether documentation is understandable and usable. Technical writers provide feedback to product developers and therefore make a significant contribution to costumer satisfaction.

Technical writers help reinforce the corporate image

Documentation is an integral part of a product. Qualified technical writers ensure that this documentation reinforces the corporate brand and image. Because technical writers may often be involved in the translation and localisation processes, they help create a positive image in all target markets.

DOCUMENTATION AND USERS

What users want from documentation

Users need documentation. For most users, the documentation is the main way to get to know products. Documentation allows users to install and use products efficiently and safely. In addition, documentation helps users solve problems while using the product, often know as troubleshooting.

A survey conducted while performing research for this guideline showed that users want high quality documentation. Documentation should have a clear layout and design, and a logical structure. It should be clearly written and the answers to specific questions should be easy to find. The documentation should describe the product features and how to use the product. The documentation should not be a list of technical features. For technically experienced users and for installation, there should be a quick reference guide with the main features.

In addition, users want efficient support. They need individual assistance when they have problems that cannot be solved with the documentation.

Public opinion about documentation

A new product is always a new task for a user. Unfortunately, users usually do not look at the documentation when buying products. Choices are often made on price and product features. Problems appear later, when the product is installed or used.

At this stage, users discover whether the documentation is useful or not. A large number of features make it difficult to use a product. The more features a product has, the more good documentation is required.

Without good documentation, users feel frustrated and helpless. They give up trying to use the relevant product features or try to find help via help lines or retailers, often in vain. Whenever people start talking about documentation, they have many stories to tell about their bad experiences.

The complicated interrelationship of manufacturers, retailers and users does not help to improve the image of documentation. It is the task of manufacturers and retailers to tackle this problem and to respond to the demands for better documentation expressed by users. It would be helpful if copies of the documentation were available at the point of sale.

AIM AND CONTENTS OF THIS GUIDELINE

Reliable minimum requirements for documentation

This guideline aims to help those responsible for documentation to assess the quality of the documentation they produce, to avoid mistakes and to create good documentation. The audience includes managers and technical writers.

This guideline is not a textbook or handbook for technical documentation and cannot replace such works. This guideline provides reliable minimum requirements for user-friendly documentation and basic information on legal issues.

Contents of this guideline

The three chapters of this guideline answer three main questions faced by those responsible for documentation.

- Does our documentation meet legal requirements?
- Does it meet the demands of users?
- Is our process organisation efficient?

Each chapter is concise and clear to help you find the information you need quickly and easily.

In addition, this guideline provides you with a collection of links to relevant European Union directives and European Council resolutions at the end. There are also links to international, European and national standards organisations, and European technical communications organisations.

This guideline is for all companies

Many manufacturers in Europe are small and medium-sized enterprises. They face special challenges when it comes to producing documentation. They often do not have the time, money or qualified staff to meet all the legal requirements and required product and consumer protection standards, such as CE marks.

As with large companies, small and medium-sized enterprises also should be aware that good documentation is an integral part of any product. Therefore, they should invest the necessary means and resources in its production. If small and medium-sized enterprises cannot afford to employ qualified staff, they can alternatively outsource their documentation projects to a qualified service provider. Most organisations for technical communication in Europe have databases with service providers and freelancers on their Web sites where a suitable business partner can be found.

Good documentation is an important factor in competing internationally. One of the main assets of European products is their high quality. High quality documentation is an inseparable and indispensable part of this asset. Documentation contributes to gaining and keeping the confidence of customers.

1. LEGAL ISSUES AND DOCUMENTATION

This chapter contains two sections. The first section contains information on how legal considerations affect documentation, including a particular focus on documentation's role as part of the product. The second section contains some steps that help you address these legal considerations.

1.1 BASIC LEGAL CONSIDERATIONS

This section contains information on the legal aspects of the following points:

- Customers require documentation
- Documentation and hazards
- Inadequate documentation leads to loss of marketability
- Companies as a whole are responsible for documentation
- Requirements and standards for translation

1. Legal Issues and Documentation

1.1.1 Customers Require Documentation

Motivation

Customers are entitled to demand contractual commitments that meet their requirements from suppliers, including having documentation in a particular language. Under European legal systems, there is also a statutory duty to include product instructions that enable customers to install and operate the product, regardless of whether this is stated in the contract. The standard to be met is a customer's expectation based on the product description, the representations of the seller and the general standards for technical documentation. If these duties are not complied with, customers have the right to refuse payment, demand improvements at the cost of the seller or seek damages. Distributors are entitled to be indemnified by the manufacturer for such claims raised by customers.

Good technical documentation must therefore be sensitive to customer requirements, anticipate them, and incorporate them as far as possible.

Action points

- ☐ Standardise the contractual basics.
- ☐ Centralise work on contracts and use experienced staff.
- ☐ Check product requirements against the technical documentation.
- ☐ Familiarise your technical writer with the contractual requirements.
- ☐ Have your technical writer review the technical documentation for compliance with the contractual requirements.
- ☐ Have the technical staff interact with the contract management staff if the technical documentation does not comply with the contractual requirements.
- ☐ Involve the technical staff in the contracts process.

Tips

- ✗ Have legal and technical staff cooperate to develop standards for contracts for the technical documentation.
- ✗ Before agreeing to a customer's request to deviate from these standards, require the contract management staff to obtain the consent of the technical staff. One possible response is to refuse to make the change.

Example

A customer orders goods in his local language and receives a confirmation from the manufacturer in the same language. The terms of business are expressed in the local language. The customer is entitled to technical documentation that is translated into his local language without a specific provision in the contract requiring this.

References

- ◆ Directive 99/44/EC of the European Parliament and of the Council of 25 May 1999 on certain aspects of the sale of consumer goods and associated guarantees
- ◆ National contract laws; e.g., for Germany: Civil Code (BGB) §§ 434 et seq.
- ◆ Case law on national contract laws
- ◆ Council Resolution of 17 December 1998 on operating instructions for technical consumer goods

1.1.2 Documentation and Hazards

Motivation

Documentation cannot compensate for poor design. Hazards that arise from use of a product must be avoided. Failure to avoid such hazards may result in the manufacturer, product labeller, importer, and dealer facing damage compensation claims from consumers. This results in a potentially large risk of litigation because in the event of damages being found, the defect is usually contained in production runs with many thousands of items.

Consumers are entitled to expect that hazards that may arise from a product have been considered and prevented in the design stage. If this is not possible, the remaining hazards can be reduced with the help of technical documentation, such as by using warnings. Attempting to minimise a hazard that is avoidable through better design with warnings leads to liability for insufficient warnings or defective design.

Action points

- ☐ State in the design specification and guidelines that potential hazards of the product are to be avoided by design measures.
- ☐ Conduct risk analyses throughout the design phase.
- ☐ Evaluate the hazards found in the risk analyses in order to eliminate them in the design phase.
- ☐ Inform the technical staff of unavoidable hazards.
- ☐ Review unavoidable hazards and act to minimise their risk by using warnings and instructions, in particular with respect to product use and misuse.
- ☐ Direct the technical staff to inform the design staff if the hazards cannot be minimised by warnings and instructions.

Tips

- ✗ Before bringing a product to market, review whether all possibilities for preventing defects have been exhausted in the product design process.
- ✗ Use focus groups consisting of non-specialist users in particular with respect to the misuse of products. Also test the interaction of instructions with the design.

Example

The manufacturer of a toy ball attaches an elastic band to it, which allows the ball to be used as a "Punching Ball". The ball is also intended for use by small children. A warning on the packaging states that the elastic band should not be over-stretched and in particular warns against pulling the band back towards the face.

A child is injured when he pulls so violently on the elastic band that it breaks off from the ball. The loop that connects the ball to the band strikes the child in his eye, severely damaging it. The court rules against the manufacturer. Despite the warning on the packaging, the manufacturer is liable for the damage because the separation of the elastic band could have been prevented by a better loop design.

References

- ◆ Directive 85/374/EEC of 25 July 1985 on the approximation of the laws, regulations and administrative provisions of the Member States concerning liability for defective products
- ◆ Directive 98/37/EC of the European Parliament and of the Council of 22 June 1998 on the approximation of the laws of the Member States relating to machinery

1. Legal Issues and Documentation

- ❖ National legislation implementing Directive 85/374/EEC of 25 July 1985 on the approximation of the laws, regulations and administrative provisions of the Member States concerning liability for defective products
- ❖ National liability laws (e.g., for Italy: Art. 2056 ff. Civil Code and/or DPR 1988/224
- ❖ Case law on EC product liability and member state liability law regimes
- ❖ Report of the EC-Commission dated 31 January 2001 on the application of Directive 85/374/EEC on liability for defective products (KOM (2000) 893)
- ❖ Council Resolution of 17 December 1998 on operating instructions for technical consumer goods

1.1.3 Inadequate Documentation Leads to Loss of Marketability

Motivation

All governments pursue the goal of protecting the health of their consumers. To accomplish this goal, governments regulate product safety and keep unsafe products away from consumers.

The European Union uses the New Approach to technical harmonisation and the Global Approach to conformity assessment with the introduction of the CE-mark to pursue this goal. Specific products, such as toys, have to meet essential safety requirements that are specified in EU directives. Among the requirements, there is a requirement for technical documentation. If a product fails to meet these requirements, it loses its marketability. This may lead to the product being removed from the market.

In the absence of explicit essential safety requirements in EU directives, EU member states apply the general clause in the EU product safety directive that prohibits the bringing of unsafe products to the market. If technical documentation that is false or incomplete causes a safety hazard, the product loses its marketability and it can be removed from the market by a recall order or other means.

Comparable product surveillance systems with essential safety requirements also exist in countries outside the European Union.

Action points

- ☐ Inform technical staff of the areas where the product is distributed.
- ☐ Review the applicability of EU directives on product safety.
- ☐ Review the applicability of other regulations and technical standards in the distribution area.
- ☐ Check whether a public authority or other institution must test or certify the product.
- ☐ Ensure the technical documentation complies with applicable EU directives and their implementation in technical standards.
- ☐ Ensure the technical documentation complies with other applicable regulations and technical standards.
- ☐ Organise competent translation of the technical documentation insofar as this is required by EU directives or other regulations or technical standards.

Tips

- ✗ If an importer handles the importation of a product, the importer should be obligated by contract to research the requirements for product marketability and to inform the manufacturer of the results.
- ✗ If making a product marketable requires unusual efforts with respect to the technical documentation, such as their translation, there should be an agreement with the customer or the importer about who is responsible for the translation and how the costs are to be borne.

Example

A German manufacturer of television sets intends to export them to Poland. Under the Polish Language Protection Law of 7 October 1999, a translation of the technical documentation into Polish is required. The manufacturer does not research what requirements apply because it assumes that meeting German requirements is sufficient. The import of the televisions is prevented at the border. Only after the technical documentation is delivered in Polish does the shipment cross the border. The Polish distributor seeks compensation for its losses caused by the late delivery of the products.

References

- Directive 73/23/EEC of 19 February 1973 on the harmonization of the laws of Member States relating to electrical equipment designed for use within certain voltage limits
- Council Directive 87/404/EEC of 25 June 1987 on the harmonization of the laws of the Member States relating to simple pressure vessels
- Directive 88/378/EEC of 3 May 1988 on the approximation of the laws of the Member States concerning the safety of toys
- Council Directive 89/106/EEC of 21 December 1988 on the approximation of laws, regulations and administrative provisions of the Member States relating to construction products
- Directive 89/336/EEC of 3 May 1989 on the approximation of the laws of the Member States relating to electromagnetic compatibility
- Directive 89/686/EEC of 21 December 1989 on the approximation of the laws of the Member States relating to personal protective equipment
- Council Directive 90/384/EEC of 20 June 1990 on the harmonization of the laws of the Member States relating to non-automatic weighing instruments
- Council Directive 90/385/EEC of 20 June 1990 on the approximation of the laws of the Member States relating to active implantable medical devices
- Directive 92/59/EEC of 29 June 1992 on general product safety
- Directive 93/42/EEC of the European Council of 14 June 1993 concerning medical devices
- Directive 94/9/EC of the European Parliament and the Council of 23 March 1994 on the approximation of the laws of the Members States concerning equipment and protective systems intended for use in potentially explosive atmospheres
- Directive 94/25/EC of the European Parliament and of the Council of 16 June 1994 on the approximation of the laws, regulations and administrative provisions of the Member States relating to recreational craft
- Directive 95/16/EC of the European Parliament and of the Council of 29 June 1995 on the approximation of the laws of the Member States relating to lifts
- Directive 97/23/EC of the European Parliament and of the Council of 29 may 1997 on the approximation of the laws of the Member States concerning pressure equipment
- Directive 98/37/EC of the European Parliament and of the Council of 22 June 1998 on the approximation of the laws of the Member States relating to machinery
- Directive 98/79/EC of the European Parliament and of the Council of 27 October 1998 on in vitro diagnostic medical devices
- Directive 99/5/EC of the European Parliament and of the Council of 9 March 1999 on radio equipment and telecommunications terminal equipment and the mutual recognition of their conformity
- Directive 2000/9/EC of the European Parliament and of the Council of 20 March 2000 relating to cableway installations designed to carry persons

- Directive 2001/95/EC of the European Parliament and of the Council of 3 December 2001 on general product safety (to be transposed into national legislation by 15 January 2004)
- EC member state implementation of EC directives
- Laws applicable in jurisdictions outside the European Union
- Centre de Droit de la Consommation: "The Practical Application of Council Directive 92/59/EEC on General Product Safety" (February 2000)

1.1.4 Companies as a Whole Are Responsible for Documentation

Motivation

The creation of technical documentation demands technical knowledge and professional skill. The profession of technical writer has evolved to meet this demand. Enterprises generally use specially trained technical writers or technical staff who have received additional training to develop technical documentation.

Specialisation can lead to the technical writer mistakenly being assigned exclusive responsibility for the technical documentation. However, this ignores the legal framework, which imposes liability for defective technical documentation on the entire company. Management must organise an environment that ensures the correct preparation of technical documentation. The appointment of a technical writer does not eliminate this organisational responsibility of management. Instead, management is required to carefully select and supervise the person appointed as technical writer.

Action points

- ☐ Assess the nature and manner of technical documentation needed for the products.
- ☐ Develop requirements for producing technical documentation based on your assessment.
- ☐ Define the general, organisational and professional requirements for the creation of technical documentation.
- ☐ Define the general and organisational requirements that are the responsibility of management.
- ☐ Separate professional requirements into personal qualifications and job requirements.
- ☐ Use the personal qualifications to search for suitable candidates for the position of technical writer.
- ☐ Use the job requirements in drawing up work instructions for technical writers.

Tips

- ✗ Retain external consultants to assess what technical documentation is necessary for the products if your company staff lack the technical expertise to accomplish this task.
- ✗ Regularly review the job description and work instructions and allow for the possibility of ad hoc reviews when essential changes occur in the product stream.

Example

A machine parts manufacturer ordinarily produces only components for machines and provides a manufacturer's declaration in accordance with the EU Machinery Directive. At the request of a customer, the manufacturer accepts an order to deliver a completely assembled machine. Shortly before delivery, it is discovered that the technical documentation required by the EU Machinery Directive does not exist. The Research and Development manager who is responsible for the design prepares documentation that consists of little more than the design drawings. For example, important warnings on safety precautions are missing. The assembled machine is delivered, and misuse occurs as a result of the inadequate instructions. The manufacturer is sued for the resulting damages. The management of the manufacturer wishes to limit responsibility to the Research and Development manager as the responsible individual. The court nonetheless holds the company liable on the grounds that the management should have better clarified how the work would be done in order to provide satisfactory technical documentation.

References

- Directive 85/374/EEC of 25 July 1985 on the approximation of the laws, regulations and administrative provisions of the Member States concerning liability for defective products
- National legislation implementing Directive 85/374/EEC of 25 July 1985 on the approximation of the laws, regulations and administrative provisions of the Member States concerning liability for defective products
- National liability laws
- Case law on EU product liability and member state liability law regimes
- Applicable EU Directives

1. Legal Issues and Documentation

1.1.5 Requirements and Standards for Translations

Motivation

Technical documentation informs users of potential hazards in handling products. To accomplish its purpose, the documentation must be comprehensible. Comprehensibility includes a sufficient amount of content, structured in a manner attuned to potential users and their knowledge. It also means using language that is understood by the readers. Therefore, it may be necessary to translate technical documentation into other languages for users.

Product safety law; for example, the EU Machinery Directive, contains some provisions that require instructions to be translated into the language of the country where it is used.

The necessity of translating technical documentation may result not only from statutory mandates. It is possible that a translation may be required by contractual provisions. This is common particularly in the field of consumer goods. Under the EU second-hand goods directive, second-hand consumer goods must have an assembly guide when consumers have to assemble the product before using it. The assembly instructions, including graphics, must be understandable to someone using the language of the user's country.

However, translation alone does not guarantee that the technical documentation is comprehensible. Especially in the consumer goods field, it may be necessary to make adjustments to account for local customs. For example, instructions in the form of graphics and illustrations are common in Asia and are better followed than is the case in Europe. Therefore, adjustments to reflect prevailing cultural customs might be needed in addition to translation.

Action points

- ☐ Identify the area of distribution.
- ☐ Determine whether translation is required by mandatory law.
- ☐ Determine whether translation is agreed by contract.
- ☐ Secure competent translation if translation is decided on.
- ☐ Ascertain local customs in the area of distribution from local companies, such as distributors.
- ☐ Ensure that local customs are considered in the translation process.

Tips

- ✗ Contracts may contain an agreement that the importer undertakes the translation, not the exporter. This may be advantageous where the importer has good technical knowledge and can more easily ascertain local customs.
- ✗ Organisational measures need to be undertaken to ensure that the translator always uses the latest version of the technical documentation. When changes are made in the technical documentation, the translation must also be revised.

Example

A German manufacturer of infant toys wishes to export them to France. It retains a distributor for this purpose, and the first orders are accepted. The infant toys are delivered with instructions in German. The local authorities in France instruct the local distributor to halt sales of the product with German instructions, citing the consumer law that requires instructions to be in French. The manufacturer must prepare French instructions and ship the products already delivered back to Germany in order to replace the German version with a French one.

References

- National liability laws
- Case law on EC product liability and member state liability law regimes
- IEC 62079: Preparation of instructions: Structuring, contents and presentation
- Council Resolution of 17 December 1998 on operating instructions for technical consumer goods

1. Legal Issues and Documentation

1.2 HOW TO TAKE LEGAL CONSIDERATIONS INTO ACCOUNT

This section contains information on the steps you need to take to address basic legal considerations in your documentation.

The following actions are described:

- Collect the legal requirements to be able to meet customer requirements
- Conduct risk analyses
  As result of the risk analyses:
    - Use effective warnings to disclose hazards
    - Highlight warnings with standardised safety graphics
    - Ensure warnings are effective by prioritising them
    - Include warnings against product misuse
    - Ensure that technical documentation is kept up-to-date
- Monitor compliance with current developments to keep the product marketable
- Plan for international distribution

1.2.1 Collect the Legal Requirements

Motivation

You need to ensure that you meet customer requirements, that you are not held liable for damages, and that your products remain on the market.

The best way to do this is to research the legal requirements for technical documentation in each jurisdiction that a particular product is distributed in. List the results in a guide containing the requirements for technical documentation. To conduct such research, it is necessary to define precisely the product, its characteristics, the target user group, the intended use, and the area of distribution.

Action points

- ☐ Define the product.
- ☐ Define the product's characteristics.
- ☐ Define the target user group.
- ☐ Define the intended use of the product.
- ☐ Define the area of distribution.
- ☐ Research the legal requirements.
- ☐ Keep the legal requirements updated to include periods up to market entry.
- ☐ Ensure the guide is updated when legal requirements change.

Tips

- ✗ Use external service providers to research legal requirements for areas where distribution experience is lacking.
- ✗ Use Research and Development work to get information on the product, product characteristics, target group and product use.

Example

A manufacturer of kitchen appliances instructs its technical staff to develop technical documentation in English when it gets an order from a customer located in the USA-Mexico border area. The manufacturer neglects to prepare a guide on the creation of technical documentation. The product is delivered. However, the technical documentation does not comply with the applicable ANSI and Mexican standards, there is no Spanish translation, and it does not address American or Mexican usage patterns. A user is injured when using the appliance in an improper manner; further distribution is prohibited. The importer claims damages from the manufacturer.

References

- ◈ Directive 85/374/EEC of 25 July 1985 on the approximation of the laws, regulations and administrative provisions of the Member States concerning liability for defective products
- ◈ National legislation implementing Directive 85/374/EEC of 25 July 1985 on the approximation of the laws, regulations and administrative provisions of the Member States concerning liability for defective products
- ◈ National liability laws
- ◈ Case law on EC product liability and members states liability law regimes
- ◈ Laws applicable in jurisdictions outside the European Union

1. Legal Issues and Documentation

1.2.2 Conduct Risk Analyses

Motivation

To ensure that there is no liability for damages, it is necessary to avoid potential product hazards in the design phase. The remaining unavoidable design hazards must be explained to the user through references in the technical documentation.

Accidents can best be avoided by awareness of potential hazards. Risk analyses must precede the creation of technical documentation to minimise hazards. Technical documentation that is prepared without a risk analysis cannot minimise hazards and does not fulfil the reasonable safety expectations of product users.

Action points

- ☐ Define the user groups.
- ☐ Analyse the knowledge of the user groups.
- ☐ Evaluate the knowledge of the least educated and least trained user group.
- ☐ Define the knowledge of the average user of the user group with the weakest qualifications.
- ☐ Evaluate the remaining environmental conditions, such as operating temperatures.
- ☐ Evaluate the product for hazards under conditions of proper use.
- ☐ Evaluate the product for hazards under conditions of foreseeable product misuse.

Tips

- ✗ Follow the principles described in the Documentation and Hazards section. Risk analysis should be conducted during the product development and where possible, at every stage of development. Design the product to avoid hazards where possible.
- ✗ Consider the following in your risk analyses: knowledge from previous products, experience gained in the manufacturing process, and experience from market surveillance and the handling of customer complaints.

Example

A manufacturer of products for mountain biking has introduced a special light handlebar to the market. In normal everyday use, there are no difficulties. However, use of the handlebar under racing conditions by semi-professional bicyclists can result in the bar snapping. The handlebar is provided in a manner where only users with semi-professional knowledge and experience are able to install it. The manufacturer was sued and held liable for damages. The court held that there should have been a warning on the limited use of the handlebar in semi-professional sporting conditions. A risk analysis would have disclosed the necessity of a warning.

References

- ◆ EC Directive 85/374/EEC of 25 July 1985 on the approximation of the laws, regulations and administrative provisions of the Member States concerning liability for defective products
- ◆ Directive 98/37/EC of the European Parliament and of the Council of 22 June 1998 on the approximation of the laws of the Member States relating to machinery

- ◈ Directive 2001/95/EC of the European Parliament and of the Council of 3 December 2001 on general product safety (to be transposed into national legislation by 15 January 2004)
- ◈ National legislation implementing 85/374/EEC of 25 July 1985 on the approximation of the laws, regulations and administrative provisions of the Member States concerning liability for defective products
- ◈ National liability laws
- ◈ Case law on EC product liability and Member State liability law regimes

1. Legal Issues and Documentation

1.2.3 Use Effective Warnings to Disclose Potential Hazards

Motivation

To ensure that there is no liability for damages, it is necessary to avoid potential product hazards in the design phase. The remaining unavoidable design hazards must be explained to the user through references in the technical documentation.

The results of a risk analysis on a product's hazards should be used in warnings that specify as much as possible the most effective way to avoid the hazard. Warnings must be easy to comprehend (both in terms of their content and in terms of the language the warning is in), easy to see and easy to get.

Only warnings that are effective in meeting these requirements can fulfil the reasonable safety expectations of users.

Action points

- ☐ Review the language levels of the user groups to ensure that all users can understand the warnings.
- ☐ Pay attention to distribution in areas using other languages.
- ☐ Do not use words in other languages and avoid technical concepts.
- ☐ Adapt the warning to the application.
- ☐ Describe the effects of the hazard that may occur.
- ☐ Describe ways to avoid hazards.
- ☐ Use graphics.
- ☐ Use standardised graphics for warnings.
- ☐ Apply warnings to the product or its packaging.
- ☐ Ensure the technical documentation accompanies the product.
- ☐ Ensure the technical documentation is clear and comprehensible.

Tips

- ✗ Use a focus group to test the technical documentation with members of the potential user group with respect to clarity, perception and availability.
- ✗ Where necessary, adjust the warnings to suit the cultural characteristics of the distribution area.

Example

> The manufacturer of a children's tea, a product common in Germany, placed a warning that continual use of the sweetened product could result in health problems. This warning was placed in the description of the contents of the tea and on the packaging of the tea without special highlighting. The claim for damages against the manufacturer was successful.

References

- ◆ Directive 85/374/EEC of 25 July 1985 on the approximation of the laws, regulations and administrative provisions of the Member States concerning liability for defective products

- Directive 2001/95/EC of the European Parliament and of the Council of 3 December 2001 on general product safety (to be transposed into national legislation by 15 January 2004)
- National legislation implementing Directive 85/374/EEC of 25 July 1985 on the approximation of the laws, regulations and administrative provisions of the Member States concerning liability for defective products
- National liability laws
- Case law on EC product liability and Member State liability law regimes
- IEC 62079: Preparation of instructions, Structuring, contents and presentation
- ISO 7010 (October 2003) Graphical symbols – Safety colours and safety signs – Safety signs used in workplaces and public areas
- ISO 3864-1 (May 2002) Graphical symbols – Safety colours and safety signs – Part 1: Design principles for safety signs in workplaces
- Council Resolution of 17 December 1988 on operating instructions for technical consumer goods

1. Legal Issues and Documentation

1.2.4 Highlight Warnings with Standardised Safety Graphics

Motivation

The overriding principle for technical documentation is to inform users of a product of potential hazards associated with its use in the most effective manner possible. Warnings are indispensable to achieve this objective. However, simply underlining or highlighting the text of hazard warnings does not suffice in every case to draw the attention of product users to potential hazards.

Warnings need to be accompanied by illustrative graphics that use standardised safety graphics. For example, it is insufficient to rely on a mere textual reference that a product is acidic and its use requires protective measures to avoid injury. Such a reference would not absolutely lead users to exercise appropriate care in all situations. A symbol on the product packaging illustrating acid dropping on a hand with the resulting injuries is far more effective in getting users to adjust their behaviour.

A range of expertise in the form of technical standards is available when using safety graphics. However, the internationalisation of such safety graphics remains limited in scope. It is important to note regional differences in standardised safety graphics, particularly those common in Europe on the one hand and in the United States of America on the other. In using safety graphics, care must be taken to observe regional variances.

Action points

- ☐ Identify safety graphics and the situations where they are needed.
- ☐ Check that textual descriptions of safety hazards are complete.
- ☐ Choose appropriate safety graphics to accompany or be used in lieu of textual descriptions.
- ☐ Check whether technical standards prescribe particular safety graphics.
- ☐ Determine whether regional variations exist.
- ☐ Implement warning symbols to reinforce the warnings in the text.
- ☐ Test the safety graphics and the warnings for effectiveness.

Example

> The manufacturer of a paper shredder places text on its shredder that users should be careful to not put their hands into the paper feed when inserting paper. Unseen by the users, a rotating blade that can cause serious injury lies directly behind the paper feed. The potential hazard remains abstract in the text. A court grants damage compensation to an injured user because the manufacturer of the paper shredder should have used a safety graphic. For example, the court thought that users should have been warned by an illustrative graphic showing hands with big bars drawn over them at the point where the paper was fed into the machine.

References

- ◆ Directive 85/374/EEC of 25 July on the approximation of the laws, regulations and administrative provisions of the Member States concerning liability for defective products
- ◆ Directive 2001/95/EC of the European Parliament and of the Council of 3 December 2001 on general product safety (to be transposed into national legislation by 15 January 2004)

1.2 How to Take Legal Considerations into Account

- National legislation implementing Directive 85/374/EEC of 25 July on the approximation of the laws, regulations and administrative provisions of the Member States concerning liability for defective products
- National liability laws
- Case law on EC product liability and Member State liability law regimes
- IEC 62079: Preparation of instructions, Structuring, contents and presentation
- ISO 7010 (October 2003) Graphical symbols – Safety colours and safety signs – Safety signs used in workplaces and public areas
- ISO 3864-1 (May 2002) Graphical symbols – Safety colours and safety signs – Part 1: Design principles for safety signs in workplaces
- Council Resolution of 17 December 1998 on operating instructions for technical consumer goods

1. Legal Issues and Documentation

1.2.5 Ensure Warnings Are Effective by Prioritising Them

Motivation

To ensure that there is no liability for damages, it is necessary to avoid potential product hazards in the design phase. The remaining unavoidable design hazards must be explained to users through references in the technical documentation.

The results of risk analyses of potential safety hazards must be used to create effective safety warnings. Only these warnings fulfil the reasonable safety expectations of product users.

The information in the technical documentation must be prioritised. Safety graphics showing significant potential hazards have priority over safety graphics for hazards of lesser danger and/ or are less likely to occur.

Action points

- ☐ Prioritise the hazards discovered in risk analysis according to degree of risk for life and limb and property damage.
- ☐ Evaluate the probability of potential hazards occurring.
- ☐ Evaluate user knowledge of the potential hazard, its nature and likelihood.
- ☐ Evaluate apparent hazards.
- ☐ Evaluate latent hazards.
- ☐ Rank the risks. Warn of latent hazards before apparent hazards, significant hazards before minor hazards, and probable events before improbable ones.
- ☐ List safety graphics in accordance with the above ranking.
- ☐ Place safety graphics in the technical documentation in accordance with the ranking.

Tips

- ✗ Review the effectiveness of the technical documentation by using focus groups with potential users, allowing them to rank the potential hazards. Coordinate their ranking with the internally produced ranking.
- ✗ Place safety graphics on the packaging, product or both, as appropriate.

Example

The way personal watercraft equipment is manufactured means it has little buoyancy when the motor is turned off. When used for long stretches of time, it is therefore recommended that users wear a life jacket for their safety. The technical documentation for the personal watercraft equipment has a separate page with numerous safety graphics, showing in detail the hazards of using the equipment with respect to steering, speed, etc. At the end of the safety graphics, there is also a warning that the equipment is only slightly buoyant when the motor is turned off. Therefore, the wearing of a life jacket is essential. The motor fails on a personal watercraft used by a person who does not wear a life jacket while using the equipment for a long time. The user has to be rescued at sea. His health is severely damaged. The manufacturer is liable because, in view of the significant hazard and the not insignificant likelihood of its occurrence, the safety graphic about the low buoyancy of the equipment when the motor is switched off should have been more prominently placed.

References

◆ Directive 85/374/EEC of 25 July 1985 on the approximation of the laws, regulations and administrative provisions of the Member States concerning liability for defective products

◆ Directive 2001/95/EC of the European Parliament and of the Council of 3 December 2001 on general product safety (to be transposed into national legislation by 15 January 2004)

◆ National legislation implementing Directive 85/374/EEC of 25 July 1985 on the approximation of the laws, regulations and administrative provisions of the Member States concerning liability for defective products

◆ National liability laws

◆ Case law on EC product liability and member state liability law regimes

◆ IEC 62079: Preparation of instructions, Structuring, contents and presentation

◆ Council Resolution of 17 December 1988 on operating instructions for technical consumer goods

1.2.6 Include Warnings Against Product Misuse

Motivation

To ensure that there is no liability for damages, it is necessary to avoid potential product hazards in the design phase. The remaining unavoidable design hazards must be explained to users through references in the technical documentation

The results of risk analyses of potential safety hazards must be used to create effective safety warnings. Only these warnings fulfil the reasonable safety expectations of product users.

The manufacturer of a product designs it for particular uses. However, general life experience tells us that product users do not only use products for their intended purposes. Therefore, they can expect to be warned about hazards outside of the intended use and purpose of the product.

Action points

- ☐ Define the expected use of the product.
- ☐ Determine likely improper product misuse.
- ☐ Rank types of likely improper product use by probability of occurrence.
- ☐ Label unlikely improper product use as product misuse.
- ☐ Determine socially acceptable use of the product.
- ☐ Examine known product use that is not within the socially acceptable use and the likelihood of its occurrence.
- ☐ Treat surplus product as subject to being used.
- ☐ Consider improper product use in the giving of warnings.

Tip

× Evaluate product use cases with reference to improper use at regular intervals within the product life cycle. Ask distribution employees about the topic. Provide the responses to the documentation staff.

Example

An insecticide is introduced to the market that is also suitable for use in residences. The substance was tested for it effects on human health, but only when used on ornamental plants. On account of its efficacy, the insecticide is also used for fruit-bearing plants. However, ripe fruits may not come in contact with the substance because it can be harmful if ingested. The manufacturer is informed about the use on fruit plants by its sales staff, but it omits a warning on using the substance in this manner. Several users suffer damage to their health after eating fruit that had been sprayed with the substance. The manufacturer is liable for the damages.

References

- ◆ Directive 85/374/EEC of 25 July 1985 on the approximation of the laws, regulations and administrative provisions of the Member States concerning liability for defective products
- ◆ Directive 2001/95/EC of the European Parliament and of the Council of 3 December 2001 on general product safety (to be transposed into national legislation by 15 January 2004)
- ◆ National legislation implementing Directive 85/374/EEC of 25 July 1985 on the approximation of the laws, regulations and administrative provisions of the Member States concerning liability for defective products

- National liability laws
- Case law on EU product liability and member state liability law regimes
- IEC 62079: Preparation of instructions: Structuring, contents and presentation

1. Legal Issues and Documentation

1.2.7 Ensure that Technical Documentation is Kept Up-to-date

Motivation

To ensure that there is no liability for damages, it is necessary to avoid potential product hazards in the design phase. The remaining unavoidable design hazards must be explained to the user through references in the technical documentation.

Under the EU product liability directive, the time of entry on the market is used in determining the knowledge that the manufacturer is deemed to have had on potential hazards. However, case and statutory law in a number of countries also obligates manufacturers to monitor product performance in the market. If as a result of such monitoring, a manufacturer learns of inadequate warnings or other deficiencies in the technical documentation, the instructions need to be improved and the hazards reduced by the use of appropriate safety graphics.

Action points

- ☐ Ensure systematic evaluation of returns and complaints.
- ☐ Monitor the relevant trade press for information applicable to your product.
- ☐ Evaluate problems that users have presented.
- ☐ Forward information from returns, complaints and market monitoring to the design and documentation departments.
- ☐ Analyse potential hazards.
- ☐ In case of high risk, issue separate warning notices and, if necessary, recall products.
- ☐ In case of low risk, improve the technical documentation.

Tips

- ✗ Systematic evaluation is the key to product monitoring. Sporadic analysis of returns and complaints is not enough. The risk is high that by doing so you will fail to discover production defects or significant hazards to users.
- ✗ Knowledge management is the prerequisite for product monitoring. It must be intensively pursued to maintain compliance with developments in current science and technology. Information gained in this manner can be used to evaluate returns and complaints and to correctly judge market developments.

Example

> A manufacturer of accessories for diving gear brings a body suit to the market. It is designed to be used underneath a dry suit. Dry suits have an air outlet valve, which is necessary to prevent divers from having additional buoyancy. The technical press reports the hazard that the breathable body suit could possibly block the air outlet valve of the dry suit, resulting in undesired buoyancy for divers. The article in the trade press appears after the market entry of the body suits. The manufacturer is aware of the report, but fails to take action on it. An accident occurs as a result of the blockage of the air outlet valve that severely damages the health of a non-professional diver. The manufacturer is held liable The court decided that the manufacturer should have supplemented the instructions with a reference to the potential hazard of a blocked air outlet valve in particular types of dry suits.

References

- ◈ Directive 85/374/EC of 25 July on the approximation of the laws, regulations and administrative provisions of the Member States concerning liability for defective products

- National legislation implementing the 25 July Directive on the approximation of the laws, regulations and administrative provisions of the Member States concerning liability for defective products
- National liability laws
- Case law on EU product liability and Member State liability law regimes
- IEC 62079: Preparation of instructions, Structuring, contents and presentation

1. Legal Issues and Documentation

1.2.8 Monitor Compliance with Current Developments

Motivation

You need to ensure that you meet customer requirements, that you are not held liable for damages, and that your products remain on the market.

The best way to do this is to monitor developments in science and technology. Scientific developments include inventions and processes that are legally recognised but not yet tested in practice. Technological developments include inventions and processes that are scientifically recognised and tested in practice but have not yet become the general standard.

Action points

- ☐ Regularly monitor technical literature and apply it in company processes.
- ☐ Send employees for continuing education on current developments and use this knowledge in company processes.
- ☐ Review relevant technical standards and consider them when preparing technical documentation.
- ☐ Ensure familiarity and compliance with relevant technical standards.
- ☐ If technical standards are not relevant or applicable because the product has unique characteristics, state this and document it.
- ☐ Know how competing producers handle the same issues and be familiar with their product instructions, including how they handle translation.

Tips

- ✗ Build databases to which all employees in the company have access.
- ✗ Encourage employees to participate actively in professional associations concerned with the creation of technical documentation and encourage such persons to document the knowledge acquired in this manner and make it accessible within the company.

Example

The manufacturer of a paper shredder neglects to provide a graphic warning of the hazards caused by the rolling cutting edge in the product. However, the applicable work safety regulation of the Vocational Insurance Association requires that paper shredders have a graphic portraying this hazard. Following a plant inspection of a user of the shredder, an inspector from the insurance association prohibited its use. Before this occurred, an employee had his hand mangled after getting it caught in the shredder. The injured party recovered the costs of rehabilitation in a legal action against the manufacturer, plus compensation for pain and suffering.

References

- ◈ Directive 85/374/EEC of 25 July 1985 on the approximation of the laws, regulations and administrative provisions of the Member States concerning liability for defective products
- ◈ Directive 2001/95/EC of the European Parliament and of the Council of 3 December 2001 on general product safety (to be transposed into national legislation by 15 January 2004)
- ◈ National legislation implementing Directive 85/374/EEC of 25 July 1985 on the approximation of the laws, regulations and administrative provisions of the Member States concerning liability for defective products

1.2 How to Take Legal Considerations into Account

- ◈ National liability laws
- ◈ Case law on EC product liability and Member State liability law regimes
- ◈ Report of the EC-Commission of 31 January 2001 about the application of Directive 85/374/EEC of 25 July 1985 on the approximation of the laws, regulations and administrative provisions of the Member States concerning liability for defective products (KOM (2000) 893)

1. Legal Issues and Documentation

1.2.9 Plan for International Distribution

Motivation

Products, and consumable goods in particular, can be expected to be used in a variety of countries. Products manufactured in Europe are used worldwide. The nature and manner in which product users receive necessary information varies according to regional differences.

Product users in the United States of America, Europe, and Asia have different expectations and ways in which they perceive product hazards. Manufacturers need to differentiate these regional varieties and adjust their communication accordingly.

In addition, manufacturers often lack complete knowledge of the distribution area of their products. If a manufacturer is aware of the distribution area, adjustments can be expected to be made by it in the technical documentation. Otherwise, it is the responsibility of the importer to make these adjustments. These obligations should be specified in a contract. There should be a structured approach to the management of international communications for technical documentation in order to reduce the risk of liability.

Action points

- ☐ Identify the known distribution areas.
- ☐ Make appropriate adjustments in the technical documentation for these areas.
- ☐ Determine whether the structure of the technical documentation can be retained.
- ☐ Define distribution areas for customers and importers.
- ☐ Define who is responsible for adjustments to the technical documentation in particular distribution areas.
- ☐ Review international adjustments at regular intervals.

Tips

- ✗ Secure accurate information on the distribution area through close cooperation between the distribution staff and the documentation staff.
- ✗ Identify distribution areas that deviate from the common standard and ensure that the necessary adjustment of the documentation is implemented.

Example

A German manufacturer seeks to sell a hair-dryer in Asia. The Asian partner also plans to sell the product in the United States of America. The manufacturer already has a subsidiary in the United States of America. The product that is exported to Asia has instructions intended for Asian users. It is not in English or Spanish, and the safety graphics are not commonly used in the United States of America. An injury occurs in the United States of America, and the manufacturer's subsidiary there is sued. The manufacturer faces substantial liability. The manufacturer cannot demand indemnification from the Asian distributor because it was contractually bound to distribute the product only in Asia.

References

- ◈ National liability laws
- ◈ Case law on liability law regimes
- ◈ IEC 62079: Preparation of instructions, Structuring, contents and presentation

2. BASICS OF USER FRIENDLY DOCUMENTATION

The term user friendliness has many definitions. One general approach is to define user friendliness as the ease with which users can achieve specific tasks with documentation in an effective, efficient and safe manner. Terms such as usability and approachability are often used to indicate the same property. In essence the key is to create documentation that helps users achieve their goals, without placing undue demands upon them.

This chapter provides information on the following topics:

- Analysing who you write for before you start creating documentation
- Information usually contained in documentation
- Basic characteristics of good documentation

2.1 ANALYSING WHO YOU WRITE FOR

Before you begin creating documentation, you need to have an understanding of your audience's needs to know what characteristics your documentation should have.

This section provides information on the following topics

- Target audience analysis in order to define who the document is being written for
- Internationalisation in order to create documentation in a manner that minimises problems when translating and/or localising it for other audiences.

2.1.1 Target Audience Analysis

Motivation

Good technical documentation addresses users in an appropriate manner and takes their circumstances into account. In order to achieve this goal, a target audience analysis should be performed.

Analysing the target audience allows you to find out who the users are and what information they need to properly use the product without hurting themselves or causing damage. Audience characteristics include the technical knowledge they possess, their relationship to the product, the ease with which they use the product, educational background, and preferences in the delivery of information.

Action points

- ☐ Prepare a list of all the types of users who will use the product.
- ☐ Classify users according to their background/experience and how they use the product.
- ☐ Draw up user profiles that contain details on user characteristics that may affect how they use the application. Consider:
    - o How well do they understand the application?
    - o What experience do they have of similar applications?
    - o Are they likely to have any specialist knowledge or skills?
- ☐ Clarify the type of information users need at different stages by analysing the way the performance of users of each type changes over time as they learn about and use the application. Consider the following stages:
    - o Learning to use the product.
    - o Using the product occasionally or frequently.
    - o Using the product.
    - o Exploiting advanced features.
- ☐ Collect details on user working environments to decide the most convenient medium for presenting information to users. Consider factors that influence decisions about the types of document to provide:
    - o Is the product used in dirty, dusty or oily environments?
    - o Where will the documents be stored?

Tips

- ✗ Contact your marketing/sales department, help line staff, customer organisations, and/or your retail operations and ask them who uses the product.
- ✗ Use statistics to keep track of the customers.
- ✗ Use focus groups where possible.
- ✗ Picture yourself as a customer: what do you use the product for, how do you use it, what do you need to know, what information do you want to read in the document?

References

- ◈ ISO/IEC FDIS 18019 Software and system engineering – Guidelines for the design and preparation of user documentation for applicable software and system engineering

⬥ IEC 62079 Preparation of instructions, Structuring, contents and presentation, section 4.7.2

2.1.2 Internationalisation

Motivation

Internationalisation can mean two things: either a step in the localisation process that separates the culture-specific issues from the core message that can be the same for all cultures, or as a way of writing documentation that is as universally appealing as economically feasible. This latter concept is often called globalisation. In globalisation, the documentation and the accompanying product have been adapted to create a kind of compromise that is adequate all over the world.

Since technical documentation is often translated and/or localised in order to meet contractual or statutory requirements, it is best to design products and their documentation in a manner that minimises potential problems during these processes. This avoids extra costs and delays in schedules.

Even if you do not plan to distribute products in areas with different languages, you may have obligations caused by a reasonable expectation of products being used in other regions.

Action points

- ☐ Be aware of your audience's cultural expectations, avoiding metaphors, sporting references and mentions of educational systems that are unfamiliar to them.
- ☐ Be aware of and enable translation of various target area conventions for expressing information such as dates, items in a list, sorting and separating decimals.
- ☐ Avoid overuse of jargon, explaining when you first use a term and add a glossary entry.
- ☐ Avoid overly complicated sentence structures.
- ☐ Define all product specific terminology, adding terms to the glossary.
- ☐ Take account of the fact that different markets use different systems of measurements and allow for the need for conversions.
- ☐ Use internationally standardised symbols where possible.
- ☐ Avoid words in pictures.
- ☐ Design your document to allow expansion or shrinkage due to translation into other languages.
- ☐ Be prepared to produce various sets of images for different target markets.
- ☐ Remember that different colours are culturally sensitive in different areas.
- ☐ Define target locales and their specific legal implications.
- ☐ Be aware that different areas have different ways of addressing the reader, and not all ways work everywhere.

Tips

- ✗ Use only pictograms that are international and cannot be misunderstood.
- ✗ Symbols must be clearly illustrated, understandable or explained
- ✗ Be aware that both the imperial and metric systems of measurements are used in the United Kingdom, and that often the metric system of measurement is not used in the United States of America.
- ✗ Consider creating separate language versions of the documentation, as users often may not like documentation containing mulitple langauges on the same page or thick documentation containing many sections with different languages.

References

◈ IEC 62079: Preparation of instructions, Structuring, contents and presentation, section 4.7.3 Language

◈ ISO 7010 (October 2003) Graphical symbols – Safety colours and safety signs – Safety signs used in workplaces and public areas

◈ ISO 3864-1 (May 2002) Graphical symbols – Safety colours and safety signs – Part 1: Design principles for safety signs in workplaces

◈ ISO 11684 (January 1995) Tractors, machinery for agriculture and forestry, powered lawn and garden equipment – Safety signs and hazard pictorials – General principles

◈ Council Resolution of 17 December 1998 on operating instructions for technical consumer goods; Chapter 5: Language of manuals

2. Basics of User Friendly Documentation

2.2 INFORMATION YOU MUST INCLUDE

Good technical documentation structures and organises information to make it comprehensible to users. This results in the documentation containing different sections with different types of information to enable users to find what they need to know quickly and easily.

This section provides a basic set of information you should consider including in your documentation. Not all products require the same solution. Sometimes you may wish to consider having all this information in one document. In this case, it may be that the information may be only one or two paragraphs long, as long as it contains all the information of that type in one place. Other times, you may wish to have separate documents for some or all of this information. For example, the product may be unusually complex and the people who need the information may be in completely different audiences. To address these needs, two different documents might be in order. However, you do need to consider including each kind of information for your product in some manner.

The sections are as follows:

- Product Description
- Safety
- Getting Started
- Operation
- Troubleshooting
- Maintenance and Service
- Spare Parts and Accessories
- Packaging, Transport and Storage
- Recycling and Disposal

2.2.1 Product Description

Motivation

The product description section contains general information about the product, its features and functions, and its appropriate use. It includes all the important information about the product and provides an overview of the technical data and the equipment, including warnings.

Action points

- ☐ Provide information on the following points:
    - Preconditions
    - Product overview
    - Product purpose
    - Warnings and hazards of product use and misuse
    - Expected working environments
    - Hazardous areas
    - Exploded diagram plan for product
    - Functional description of assemblies
    - Declarations of conformity
    - Markings on the product
    - Weights and measures
    - Supply, interfaces, connections and tank capacities
    - Environmental conditions
    - Emissions
    - Reliability
    - Product variants
    - Supplied regular accessories
    - Consumables
    - Delivery condition
    - Special accessories
    - Location of items that need to be stored
    - Performance

Tip

- ✗ Describe what you can do with the product, not how it works

References

- ◈ EN 292-2 section 5.5
- ◈ Directive 98/37/EC of the European Parliament and the Council of 22 June 1998 on the approximation of the laws of the Member States relating to machinery, Annex 1, section 1.7.4
- ◈ IEC 62079 Preparation of instructions, Structuring, contents and presentation

2.2.2 Safety

Motivation

The safety section contains dangers, warnings and cautions about hazards when using the product. While hazards should be avoided in the design phase, this may not be possible. Since users are entitled to expect that hazards arising from product use have been eliminated in the product design stage, any remaining hazards must be reduced with the help of technical documentation. Based on risk analyses, the technical documentation must clearly and effectively contain warnings about any hazards from product use and misuse. Warnings must be easy to comprehend, easy to see, and contain information about how to avoid hazards. Warnings must be associated with standardised safety graphics.

Action points

- ☐ Provide information on the following points:
    - Explanations on the presentation of safety instructions, signals and graphics
    - Requirements for operating staff
    - Intended purpose of the product, definition of appropriate product use
    - Hazard and product safety considerations
    - Warnings about hazards arising from inappropriate use
    - Expected working environments and possible hazards. Examples of possibles issues include moving parts, sharp objects and pressurised components.
    - Special product hazards
    - Security circuits
    - Safety and monitoring devices
    - Use of safety devices
    - Warnings
    - Hazards caused by operating supplies. Examples include such things as the danger of flammable liquids like gasoline.
    - Hazards when using with other products
    - Declarations of conformity
    - Accepted regulations with regard to occupational safety
    - Assistance to injured persons and first aid measures

Tip

- ✗ Conduct a risk analysis to determine hazards arising from product use and misuse.

References

- ◈ EN 292-2 section 5.5
- ◈ Directive 98/37/EC of the European Parliament and the Council of 22 June 1998 on the approximation of the laws of the Member States relating to machinery, Annex 1, section 1.7.4

2.2.3 Getting Started

Motivation

The getting started section contains information on installation, initial set-up and using the product for the first time. If specialists from the manufacturer are needed for these actions, this must be emphasised.

Action points

- ☐ Provide information on the following points:
    - ○ Safety regulations for transportation, handling and installation
    - ○ Required safety measures from users
    - ○ Transport, avoidance of damage during transport, storage and delivery verification
    - ○ Transport devices, fixing and mounting devices
    - ○ List all necessary illustrations for installation, assembly and initial set-up
    - ○ Prerequisites for power supply and operating supply items
    - ○ Handling, unpacking and cleaning
    - ○ Installation location, adjustment, setting up
    - ○ Sequence of assembly, kind and scope of work and tools
    - ○ Connections, energy supply and operating supplies
    - ○ Protective devices
    - ○ Actions before getting started

Tip

- ✗ Consider a separate sheet and/or a label on the product and/or its packaging with warnings about preconditions before installation or set-up.

References

- ◆ EN 292-2 section 5.5
- ◆ Directive 98/37/EC of the European Parliament and the Council of 22 June 1998 on the approximation of the laws of the Member States relating to machinery, Annex 1, section 1.7.4
- ◆ IEC 62079 Preparation of instructions, Structuring, contents and presentation

2.2.4 Operation

Motivation

The operation section contains information on the safe operation of the product. This includes clear and comprehensible instructions on safely using all the features of the product in a manner that meets customer expectations.

Action points

- ☐ Provide information on the following points:
    - ○ Detailed warnings on particular hazards
    - ○ Note on appropriate use and use restrictions
    - ○ Requirements for those operating the product
    - ○ Data input, programming
    - ○ Checks before switching the product on
    - ○ Switching the product on
    - ○ Using the product
    - ○ Monitoring, controls
    - ○ Switching the product off
    - ○ Moving the product

Tips

- ✗ Describe average tasks that the product is used for.
- ✗ Present steps in a logical order.

References

- ❖ EN 292-2 section 5.5
- ❖ Directive 98/37/EC of the European Parliament and the Council of 22 June 1998 on the approximation of the laws of the Member States relating to machinery, Annex 1, section 1.7.4
- ❖ IEC 62079 Preparation of instructions, Structuring, contents and presentation

2.2.5 Troubleshooting

Motivation

The troubleshooting section contains information that allows users to identify problem situations and decide what can be safely done by themselves and what requires the assistance of a specialist to correct the situation. This section often includes frequently asked questions (FAQs) lists, steps to diagnose the problem and instructions on safely correcting the problem. In complex systems, there may be fault trees and computer-based fault diagnosis. The content of the section depends on the risk analyses, the audience analysis and the evaluation of what users can reasonably expect.

The location, diagnosis, and correction of problems must be limited to those tasks that users can reasonably be expected to undertake without any hazard.

Action points

- ☐ Start with safety precautions and warnings related to problem detection and troubleshooting.
- ☐ Provide clear instructions on whether users should attempt to troubleshoot themselves or whether they should consult qualified service staff.
- ☐ Create instructions for identifying and locating problems, including abnormal symptoms.
- ☐ List messages, cautions and warnings provided by the product, and how they may be recorded if appropriate.
- ☐ Create instructions for identifying normal operation.
- ☐ Describe built-in diagnostic systems that aid detection of problems, when applicable.
- ☐ Create instructions for starting standby or alternative systems, and for shutting-down and isolating malfunctioning units, if appropriate.
- ☐ Provide contact information for the supplier or other sources of technical assistance.
- ☐ List the information users should have if they contact the supplier or some other technical assistance centre.

Tips

- ✗ Contact your technical division and ask for indicators of problem situations and information on any possible built-in fault diagnosis system.
- ✗ Contact your marketing/sales department, help line staff, and service centre and ask what they know about the intended users.
- ✗ Make sure to limit the tasks to those that users could reasonably be expected to undertake without any hazard.

Reference

- ◇ IEC 62079 Preparation of instructions, Structuring, content and presentation, Section 5.10.5

2.2.6 Maintenance and Service

Motivation

The maintenance section contains information required for the care of the product. This includes recommendations, references and appropriate instructions to guarantee safe care and cleaning by the user.

Action points

- ☐ Give information on the following points:
    - ○ Hazards warnings
    - ○ Dangers during disassembly or ramping down
    - ○ Consequences when instructions are not carried out as they are described
    - ○ Instructions for cleaning
    - ○ Cleaning materials
    - ○ Consequences, if instructions on cleaning and materials are not followed
    - ○ Frequency of cleaning and maintenance
    - ○ Notes on service stations or authorised service staff
    - ○ Contact information for service or maintenance staff/companies/agencies

Tips

- ✕ When indicating a service number, provide instructions for users on what information they need to provide and where they can find it.
- ✕ Consider whether you should have a warning that the product should not be opened due to a lack of user-servicable parts inside or dangers caused by high voltage, even if the product is not plugged in.

References

- ◆ EN 292-2 section 5.5
- ◆ Directive 98/37/EC of the European Parliament and the Council of 22 June 1998 on the approximation of the laws of the Member States relating to machinery, Annex 1, section 1.7.4
- ◆ IEC 62079 Preparation of instructions, Structuring, contents and presentation, section 5.11

2.2.7 Spare Parts and Accessories

Motivation

The spare parts and accessories section contains information on what spare parts and accessories are available for the product. There should be enough information to allow users to easily identify and order the spare part of accessory required. In addition, this information helps service staff to repair the product. However, this section does not provide repair instructions. The spare parts and accessories lists should contain graphics, numbers lists, and alphabetical parts lists.

Action points

- ☐ Provide information on the following points:
    - Different variants
    - Definition of abbreviations
    - Diagrams
    - Reference list for the easy location of the components
    - Where spare parts and accessories can be purchased

References

- ◈ EN 292-2 section 5.5
- ◈ Directive 98/37/EC of the European Parliament and the Council of 22 June 1998 on the approximation of the laws of the Member States relating to machinery, Annex 1, section 1.7.4
- ◈ IEC 62079 Preparation of instructions, Structuring, contents and presentatin, section 5.12

2. Basics of User Friendly Documentation

2.2.8 Packaging, Transport and Storage

Motivation

The packaging, transport and storage section contains information on how to store the product and its components, spare parts and operating supplies. This section provides information about preparation for storage, how to store the product without damaging it and how to start it after storage.

Action points

- ☐ Provide information on the following points:
    - Safety instructions
    - How to store the product
    - How long the product can be stored for
    - Space requirements
    - Required physical conditions for storage, such as temperature, humidity, etc.
    - Regulations/standards
    - Preparation for shutting down the product
    - Shutting down the product
    - Cleaning the product
    - Installation of any transport devices
    - Packaging
    - Labelling
    - How to ship the product
    - Removal of the packaging/the transport devices
    - Getting started after storage

Tip

- ✕ For hazardous products put labels on the product and/or the product packaging.

References

- ◈ EN 292-2 section 5.5
- ◈ Directive 98/37/EC of the European Parliament and the Council of 22 June 1998 on the approximation of the laws of the Member States relating to machinery, Annex 1, section 1.7.4
- ◈ IEC 62079 Preparation of instructions, Structuring, contents and presentation, section 5.9

2.2.9 Recycling and Disposal

Motivation

The recycling and disposal section contains information on disposing the product properly and in a non-polluting way.

Action points
- ☐ Provide information on the following points, if applicable:
    - Safety regulations and hazards warnings
    - Disposal of packaging
    - Disposal of consumables
    - Disposal of the product
    - Material categories
    - Disassembly
    - Intermediate storage of still usable assemblies
    - Return to manufacturer

Tips
- ✗ Make the user aware of environmental hazards stemming from improper use and disposal of your product.
- ✗ Have your delivery organisation/distributor provide you with information about the various national practices and legal requirements on the proper disposal of your product in your target markets.

References
- ◈ EN 292-2 section 5.5
- ◈ Directive 98/37/EC of the European Parliament and the Council of 22 June 1998 on the approximation of the laws of the Member States relating to machinery, Annex 1, section 1.7.4
- ◈ IEC 62079 Preparation of instructions, Structuring, contents and presentation, section 5.15

2. Basics of User Friendly Documentation

2.3 BASIC CHARACTERISTICS OF GOOD DOCUMENTATION

This section provides information on some of the basic characteristics of good documentation. Good documentation structures and organises information to make it comprehensible to users. Documentation is seldom read from cover to cover and almost always is read to complete a specific task. For these reasons, the information must be concise, easily understood and quickly accessible. Consider this information and ask yourself how well your documentation addresses these needs.

The characteristics of good documentation include:

- Completeness
- Useful structure
- Clear content
    - Legibility/Readability
    - Accessible by all
    - Clear terminology
- Helpful pictures and diagrams
- Appropriate output media

2.3 Basic Characteristics of Good Documentation

2.3.1 Completeness

Motivation

Users are entitled to technical documentation that provides all the information they require to operate the product in a safe manner, including installation. All the information the user requires to use the product must be present. Guarantee and warranty information should also be included.

Action points

- ☐ Include a section that states who the document is for and what users need to know.
- ☐ Organise information logically in a manner that reflects safe and practical use.
- ☐ Clearly separate safety instructions, cautions and warnings, installation instructions and instructions for use.
- ☐ Include information on safety aspects.
- ☐ Make sure warnings are clearly visible on the packaging and product label to ensure that users see the warnings before they use the product.
- ☐ Follow international standards for warnings.
- ☐ If there are mulitple versions of the product, create documentation for each version.

Tips

- ✗ Use the sample checklist in IEC 62079 Annex B.3 to make sure that you have fulfilled all requirements for your documentation.
- ✗ Have a team of reviewers read your document to make sure that it is complete.

References

- ◈ IEC 62079 Preparation of instructions, Structuring, content and presentation, Annex B and C
- ◈ IEC 62079 Preparation of instructions, Structuring, content and presentation, Annex D.3 for a sample table of contents
- ◈ Council Resolution of 17 December 1998 on operating instructions for technical consumer goods; Chapter 2: Overview over elements of content.

2. Basics of User Friendly Documentation

2.3.2 Useful Structure

Motivation

Good technical documentation is structured in the best and most appropriate manner to deliver information efficiently to users.

Good design saves time when creating documentation and makes it easier for users to find what they need. A logical order means having frequently performed tasks before less frequently performed ones, having new information before known information, or having basic information before advanced information. Information should be divided into sections and subsections, with each having a title that indicates the content of the section.

Action points

- ☐ Use a logical structure.
- ☐ Use headings.
- ☐ Create a template for the layout of your document.
- ☐ Define a template for your graphics to make graphics of a given type look similiar.
- ☐ Create a table of contents and other lists, such as lists of tables and figures, if required.
- ☐ Create indexes, if required.
- ☐ Use techniques to help users find the correct information quickly, such as headers and footers, tabs, bleeding tabs, chapter level content lists and other similar solutions.

Tips

- ✗ The better the structure, the better the information can be understood.
- ✗ Simplify the layout as much as you can.
- ✗ Too many hierarchical subdivisions within the table of content can confuse users. For example, do not use headings lower than heading three (x.x.x).
- ✗ Documents longer than 20 pages should have an index.
- ✗ Avoid too many cross-references.
- ✗ An index should have at least one double-columned page for every 20 pages of text.

References

- ◇ Council Resolution of 17 December 1998 on operating instructions for technical consumer goods
- ◇ IEC 62079 Preparation of instructions, Structuring, content and presentation: Annex C

2.3.3 Clear Content

Motivation

Users are entitled to comprehensible technical documentation that meets their reasonable expectations. Comprehensible information means that it is presented in a manner that users can be reasonably expected to understand.

Content creation should result in documentation that is easily read by the target audience, which means communicating with them in the manner they expect. Based on risk and audience analyses, efficient warnings about hazards are required, along with accompanying international safety graphics.

Action points

- [ ] Use clear, concise, easy-to-understand, consistent, and everyday language.
- [ ] Use tables and lists where appropriate.
- [ ] Use bold text, italics and colours consistently.
- [ ] Break down tasks into steps in an appropriate manner.
- [ ] Place actions in steps in the order that they occur.
- [ ] Indicate if a table or a section is to be continued on another page.
- [ ] Use callouts and other navigation aids, pictures and layout to identify the various parts of the documentation to assist the user in effectively navigating the content.
- [ ] Be consistent and explain the conventions that you use.

Tips

- ✗ True creativity in writing documentation lies in organising clear, consistent, logical pieces of information together, not in flashy and complicated writing.
- ✗ Do not use too much bold text, italics or colours – a little goes a long way.
- ✗ Do not use synonyms for the same thing, use one term to describe the same thing.
- ✗ One method is to use italics to introduce new terms that are in the glossary and bold for simple emphasis.
- ✗ It is best if you try to use 12 or fewer steps in numbered step lists because this tends to make step list easier to understand.

References

- ◆ Council Resolution of 17 December 1998 on operating instructions for technical consumer goods
- ◆ IEC 62079 Preparation of instructions, Structuring, contents and presentation

2.3.4 Legibility/Readability

Motivation

In order for information to be clearly communicated, it must be clearly presented, both in the physical sense that it can be read and in the linguistic sense of being clearly written.

Action points

- ☐ Choose font sizes and styles that are clearly visible for all.
- ☐ Select line measures and spacing that enhance the clarity of the text.
- ☐ Place sufficient distance between words so that they are readable.
- ☐ Have sufficient contrast between the text and background to ensure the text can be read.
- ☐ Select paper of sufficient quality to ensure the text can be read.
- ☐ Use different fonts and sizes in a reasonable manner to ensure that the document does not look visually confusing.
- ☐ Make sure captions are easy to read.
- ☐ Use colours sparingly and consistently.
- ☐ Ensure that the general impression of the page is balanced and uncluttered.

Tips

- ✗ Have your document read by a team of reviewers to make sure it is readable.
- ✗ In general, do not use fonts smaller than 12 pt, but not higher than 14 pt.
- ✗ One widely used convention is to use sans serif fonts in titles and callouts, and serif font in normal body text.
- ✗ Legibility is when you do not impose any effort on the reader to simply read the message. Example of non-legible text: TYPOGRAPHY **IS ONE** of the *main* <u>issues</u> in legibility.

Reference

- ◈ IEC 62079 Preparation of instructions, Structuring, contents and presentation, section 6.2

2.3.5 Accessible by All

Motivation

Disabled users are entitled to be able to safely use the product, which includes the documentation. The requirements of disabled users should be taken into account during the product design process. In addition, during risk and audience analyses any additional requirements for documentation should be noted and acted upon.

Action points

- ☐ Use a font size large enough to be seen by the visually impaired, generally not lower than 12 pt.
- ☐ Consider the requirements of blind and visually impaired people.
- ☐ Bind the documentation in such a manner that it is easy to physically handle.
- ☐ Make audiotapes available.
- ☐ Use illustrations and pictures that are rich in contrast.
- ☐ Create web pages so that they can also be read by browsers that read Web pages for the visually impaired.
- ☐ Use typefaces that avoid any confusion between lower case, upper case and figures.

Tip

- × Consider binding the documentation in a manner that allows it to lie flat when opened, enabling users to have their hands free when using it.

References

- ◈ CEN/CENELEC Guide 6 (2003) "Guidelines for Standards developers to address the needs of older parsons and persons with disabilities"
- ◈ Web Content Accessibility Guidelines 1.0; W3C Recommendation (1999)
- ◈ Authoring Tool Accessibility Guidelines 1.0; W3C Recommendation (2000)
- ◈ User Agent Accessibility Guidelines 1.0; W3C Recommendation (2002)
- ◈ XML Accessibility Guidelines; W3C Working draft (2002)

2.3.6 Terminology

Motivation

Since users are entitled to technical documentation that is comprehensible to them, clear terminology must be used.

Action points

- ☐ Avoid unnecessary jargon or abbreviations.
- ☐ Define jargon, abbreviations and product-specific terminology that are unfamiliar to the audience.
- ☐ Use a style guide and/or a terminology database to keep the language consistent.
- ☐ Ensure consistent use of words within the documentation, on packaging and on product.
- ☐ Use comprehensible words that the audience is familiar with.
- ☐ Create a glossary where jargon is explained.
- ☐ Create a list of abbreviations and acronyms at the beginning of your document.

Tips

- ✗ Explain an abbreviation when it first appears.
- ✗ Clear terminology also helps to reduce problems in translation and/or localisation.

References

- ◈ DIN EN 1070, (1999): Safety of machinery – Terminology; Trilingual version EN 1070: 1998
- ◈ ISO 704 (2000): Terminology work – Principles and methods
- ◈ ISO 1087-1 (2000): Terminology work – Vocabulary – Part 1: Theory and application
- ◈ ISO 1087-2 (2000): Terminology work – Vocabulary - Part 2: Computer applications
- ◈ ISO 12200 (1999): Computer applications in terminology – Machine-readable terminology interchange format (MARTIF)
- ◈ ISO 12620 (2003): Computer applications in terminology – Data categories

2.3.7 Helpful Pictures and Diagrams

Motivation

Good technical documentation uses pictures and diagrams to communicate information in a manner that reinforces its content. Depending on the audience analyses, some target audiences may reasonably expect pictures and diagrams to be the primary form of communication. As with text, users are entitled to documentation that uses pictures and diagrams in a comprehensible manner.

Action points

- ☐ Only include the necessary information and represent only one new item of information per illustration.
- ☐ Ensure that any symbol used corresponds to commonly used pictograms, is easily recognisable and always has the same meaning.
- ☐ Use legends or numbers.
- ☐ Use colours sparing and consistently.
- ☐ Ensure that any illustration used corresponds exactly to what users see.
- ☐ When using a combination of text and illustrations, choose one of the two as the main medium throughout the documentation.
- ☐ Use a sufficient number of illustrations to allow users to go from one task to another without feeling lost.
- ☐ Support illustrations with clear and helpful captions, and a list of figures at the beginning of the documentation.
- ☐ Use graphical callouts to identify items such as task sequences, warnings and additional information.
- ☐ Size according to purpose.

Tips

- ✗ Be aware of cultural differences.
- ✗ Legends and numbers in pictures and diagrams save translation costs, as the translation of text in graphics can be complex.
- ✗ Consider using colours to show related components.

Reference

- ◈ IEC 62079 Preparation of instructions, Structuring, contents and presentation, section 6.3

2.3.8 Appropriate Output Media

Motivation

Users are entitled to technical documentation that is usable in the environment where that documentation will be used. The form the documentation takes should meet the reasonable expectations of the audience, based on analysis.

Action points

- ☐ Select the appropriate paper, taking size, orientation, and whether it is a leaflet, book or poster into consideration.
- ☐ Check the displays, labels and buttons on the product.
- ☐ Consider using a Web site.
- ☐ Consider using a CD to distribute the documentation.

Tip

- ✗ For example, if as a result of your target audience analysis you determine that the documentation is used in an oily environment, consider laminating it in wipe-clean plastic.

Reference

- ◈ IEC 62079 Preparation of instructions, Structuring, contents and presentation, section 4.6

3. PROCESS OPTIMISATION

This chapter contains ideas on how to optimise the processes you use to create documentation. Not all ideas are suited for all situations. However, it may be useful to compare the topics covered here with how you manage your documentation needs.

The sections are as follows:

- Management of documentation projects
- Supporting processes

3.1 MANAGEMENT OF DOCUMENTATION PROJECTS

Many processes go into the creation of documentation. These processes require management in order to create the documentation on budget and within the alloted schedule.

This section includes information on the following considerations:

- Goal definition
- Documentation plan
- Project monitoring
- Test plans for documentation
- Standards
- Project closure
- Post-Project monitoring

3. Process Optimisation

3.1.1 Goal Definition

Motivation

Goal definition defines what the result of a project should be. This process takes into account considerations such as how the documentation fits in the company's plan for the product. For example, high quality products that sell based on perceived value may require extra effort to produce high quality documentation.

The process also includes an analysis of legal requirements, the product, the audience, and what kind of documentation is required. Different products require different kinds of documentation, including considerations of output format (helps, online, print, embedded in user interface, training solutions (classroom, e-learning)), what tools are required to produce the format, and what languages the documentation should be in.

Action points

- ☐ Analyse the marketing strategy.
- ☐ Analyse the product.
- ☐ Analyse the legal requirements.
- ☐ Analyse the audience.
- ☐ Breakdown the tasks performed by users.
- ☐ Analyse what characteristics the final documentation should have.

Tips

- ✗ Make sure that the goal is concrete and realistic with the means to reach it.
- ✗ Make sure to keep the goal definition in mind during the whole project.

3.1.2 Documentation Plan

Motivation

Documentation plans allow goals to be reached within time, cost, quality and scope constraints. The goal is to reach the target in an orderly manner. This includes the management of people assigned to tasks in a project, their availability, evaluation of their skills to perform their tasks, required training, and contracting of service providers if needed.

Action points

- ☐ Schedule when things need to be ready.
- ☐ Define the tools, machines and software used to produce the documentation.
- ☐ Analyse what tasks need to be performed to create the documentation.
- ☐ Assign people to the tasks.
- ☐ Define the roles in the project and specify who does what.
- ☐ Analyse the risks in the project, and determine what can be done to minimise them.
- ☐ Specify how changes to the plan are to be managed.
- ☐ Specify a failure recovery plan in case something goes wrong.
- ☐ Draw up a communication plan to make sure everyone finds out the information they need to perform their tasks.
- ☐ Specify how different versions are to be managed.

Tips

- ✗ Keep your documentation plan up-to-date and use it.
- ✗ The documentation plan should be signed by all everyone in the project (marketing, product, documentation department etc.).

3. Process Optimisation

3.1.3 Project Monitoring

Motivation

Projects must be monitored continuously to ensure the outcome meets expectations. Projects often evolve as they develop, plans must be altered to conform to the new circumstances.

Action points

- ☐ Regularly review whether things are going according to plan.
- ☐ Check schedule, costs, new issues, and risks.
- ☐ Create a status report and share it with others involved in the project.
- ☐ Update the documentation plan if necessary.

Tips

- ✗ The sooner a problem is found and resolved, the more money is saved.
- ✗ The monitoring should be done by somebody who has an overall view about the documentation project and has the time to do it (for example, the documentation manager or documentation project manager).

3.1.4 Test Plans for Documentation

Motivation

Users are entitled to expect technical documentation to allow them to operate products safely and effectively.

Documentation testing plans allow problems with the documentation, and maybe the product, to be found before release. The earlier a problem is found and fixed, the less it costs to correct the problem, in time, money, and potential liability. In addition, documentation testing allows the reliability, and thus the role, of the documentation to be increased and the usability to be improved.

There are various kinds of tests that can be performed. These tests include content testing, which tests the content of the documentation for accuracy; functional testing, which tests that indexes and links work correctly; and usability testing, which tests that users can find the information they need and act on it. Documentation testing may also discover faults in the product. These results should be made available to the product testing project.

The testing plan should define how much is to be tested, how the test is to be done, and what questions are being answered, including queries on safety and environmental aspects. Tests should be defined to produce clear results. For example, documentation is often tested to see if users can follow the instructions it contains to see if they are able to perform the task being described in a safe manner.

In addition, documentation testing allows you to fulfil the legal requirements for CE-Marks and Warnings.

Action points

- ☐ Define the kind of testing to be performed.
- ☐ Define the testing methods.
- ☐ Schedule the testing.
- ☐ Design the tests and choose who performs the test.
- ☐ Find the test group and administer the test.
- ☐ Analyse, evaluate and report the test results.
- ☐ Initiate change management based on the test results and use it for continuous improvement.
- ☐ Conduct focus group testing, if possible.

Tips

- ✗ Better a small test, than no testing at all.
- ✗ The sooner a test comes in the process, the cheaper the changes are.
- ✗ Testing often find things that have been overlooked by the product designers.
- ✗ Test the documentation to avoid logical omissions and misunderstandings.
- ✗ Often a focus group of five people is sufficient to obtain reliable results.
- ✗ Find some operators or clients who will use the product and documentation.

3. Process Optimisation

References

- ◈ IEC 62079 Preparation of instructions, Structuring, contents and presentation: Annex A, B, C
- ◈ Ralf Geyer, tekom Hochschulschriften 4: Evaluation von Gebrauchsanleitungen, 2000

3.1.5 Standards

Motivation

Standards allow technical writers to maintain a high level of quality, to use the terms commonly expected in the field, and to be consistent.

Action points

- ☐ Analyse the terms that should be used.
- ☐ Use a style guide or create one to keep consistent.
- ☐ Consider integrating the information you have collected on legal issues into the style guide.
- ☐ Create a glossary of the terms used.

Tips

- ✗ Terminology analysis is a good starting point for writing.
- ✗ Use style guides to enforce consistency.

3.1.6 Project Closure

Motivation

When a project ends, the experience gained in the project should be analysed and stored for future use. The result should be a document listing the lessons learned, and suggestions for what might be done in future projects.

Action points

- ☐ Organise a final project meeting.
- ☐ Compare the estimated timetables and effort estimations to the actual ones and use them to help estimate the next project.
- ☐ Archive everything.

Tips

- ✗ Learn from mistakes: change is good.
- ✗ Learning from the past allows you to plan better in the future.

3.1.7 Post-Project Monitoring

Motivation

Under the EU product liability directive, the time of entry on the market is used in determining the knowledge that the manufacturer is deemed to have had on potential hazards. However, case and statutory law in a number of countries also obligates manufacturers to monitor product performance in the market. If as a result of such monitoring, a manufacturer learns of inadequate warnings or other deficiencies in the technical documentation, the instructions need to be improved and the hazards reduced by the use of appropriate safety graphics.

Once a project is over, post project monitoring allows any required changes to be made.

The user reaction to the documentation should also be monitored to address the issues users of the product have with the documentation, and take steps to correct problems if necessary or possible.

Action points

- ☐ Ensure the manual suits the product.
- ☐ Collect information from sales, troubleshooting and after sales service.
- ☐ Cover the whole life cycle of the product, including releases of new versions.
- ☐ Ensure usability and barrier free access.
- ☐ Create a Web site presenting regularly updated FAQs, known bugs and patches to download.
- ☐ Make improved versions of the documentation available, particularly to users who may have bought the product second-hand without the original documentation.

Tip

- ✗ Proactively work to prevent problems.

3. Process Optimisation

3.2 SUPPORT PROCESSES

This section provides information on processes that support the creation of documentation in general.

The support processes include:

- Information collection
- Feedback process
- Translation/Localisation
- Publishing

3.2.1 Information Collection

Motivation

The collection of information allows documentation to be planned and created. Technical writers must receive as much information as possible about the product, including risk analyses, how it works, release schedules, development plans, and any other information available. While technical writers may specialise in the creation of the documentation, the entire enterprise is responsible and liable for the result of the documentation creation process.

Action points

- ☐ Read project process documents.
- ☐ Collect information about the product.
- ☐ Evaluate the information.
- ☐ Examine prototypes and/or actual copies of the product.

Tips

- ✗ This is an ongoing process; collect information during the entire project.
- ✗ Interviews can be your most important source of information.
- ✗ Plan all interviews; know what information you are trying to get.
- ✗ People who have information need to allocate time for providing that information to those writing the documentation.
- ✗ Communicate your project plan for documentation to the managers of the people you are interviewing so that the managers know what you are asking for.

3.2.2 Feedback Process

Motivation

The feedback process allows technical writers to more easily improve the quality of the documentation. In addition, technical writers may be able to provide useful feedback to product designers.

Technical writers often become knowledge centres about products since they sometimes get more information from more sources. For example, translators may discover things in the translation process about the product that others miss. When technical writers organise the translation, they receive this information first.

Action points

- ☐ Collect reports of problems with the product from all parts of the company.
- ☐ Collect complaints or problems reported to help lines from customers.
- ☐ Use feedback provided from the translation of documentation.
- ☐ Collect both documentation and product test results.

Tips

- ✕ The more eyes, the better.
- ✕ All feedback is valuable.

3.2.3 Translation/Localisation

Motivation

A standard definition of translation is the process of converting written content in one language into content with the same meaning in another language. The Localization Industry Standards Association (LISA) defines localization as "the process of modifying products or services to account for differences in distinct markets", commonly including translation of texts in an appropriate manner for the target region.

Technical documentation must often be translated and/or localised in order to meet contractual or statutory requirements. Even if there is no plan to distribute products in areas with different languages, there may be obligations incurred by a reasonable expectation of products being used in other regions. Translation and localisation allows products and product information to be available in the language of the country of use.

The results of the translation and/or localisation process are more predictable when the process is planned. Translation and localisation is more than just delivering a text to a translation subcontractor. For example, translators expect enterprises to define how things like the name of the product, and other items that may not be translated or require special translation should be handled.

Action points

- ☐ Define quality standards expected of the translation.
- ☐ Select subcontractors early in the project.
- ☐ Schedule the translation process to make sure there is enough time for the document to be translated in the documentation plan.
- ☐ Sign a contract with the translator or translation agency.
- ☐ Provide brands/standards/glossary/terminology and/or data to the translators.
- ☐ Provide the text to be translated.
- ☐ Check translation schedule.
- ☐ Provide feedback to the translator, particularly if the translator will be used again.
- ☐ If a translation memory tool is used by the translator, include a request for a copy of that memory at the end of the project in the contract so that it can be used in future projects that may be done by a different translator.
- ☐ If the text changes after it has gone to translation, ensure the new text also goes to translation.

Tips

- ✗ Make sure you own the copyright for translated material.
- ✗ Assess the advantages of using translation memory systems.

References

- ◈ ÖNORM D 1200 (2000): Translation and Interpretation Services - Requirements for the service and the provision of the service
- ◈ ÖNORM D 1201 (2000): Translation and Interpretation Services – Translation contracts
- ◈ Draft ÖNORM D 1210 (2003): Requirements for technical communication and documentation services
- ◈ DIN 2345 (1998): Translation contracts

3.2.4 Publishing

Motivation

Users are entitled to technical documentation that is usable in the environment where that documentation will be used. Publishing produces the technical documentation in this format.

Action points

- ☐ Plan the publishing process at the beginning of the project, so all requirements are known.
- ☐ Check the layout to make sure the result is what is intended.
- ☐ Integrate the production of the document with the publishing requirements.
- ☐ Plan the distribution of the document.

Tips

- ✗ Involve your publishing people very early, because it prevents surprises later on.
- ✗ Consider using CD-ROMs and Web sites. The PDF file format is a common way of distributing documentation electronically.

GLOSSARY

Term	Definition
Caution	Indicates a hazard with a low level of risk which, if not avoided, could result in minor or moderate injury.
Danger	Indicates a hazard with a high level of risk which, if not avoided, will result in death or serious injury. This signalword is to be limited to the most extreme situations.
Documentation	All material used to explain a product, including operating manuals, product descriptions, installation guides, manuals and other similar documents, either electronic or printed.
FAQ	Frequently Asked Questions; lists of the most commonly asked questions about the product, and their answers.
Feature	A characteristic of a product designed to achieve some task, the reason why a user purchases the product.
Globalisation	Concept of writing document in a manner that is as universally appealing as economically feasible. The aim is to make the documentation as accessible as possible before translation and/or localisation.
Hazard	A source of danger that may lead to personal injury or death and/or damage to property. Also known as a risk.
Help line	A phone number that allows users quick access to help or customer service. Also known as a hot line, help desk or (customer) service line.
Internationalisation	The process of creating documentation or user interfaces in a manner that minimises problems when it is translated and/or localised.
Localisation	The Localization Industry Standards Association (LISA) defines localization as "the process of modifying products or services to account for differences in distinct markets", commonly including translation of texts in a manner for the target region.
Note	Information the users should pay attention to as it qualifies or amplifies other information in the document.
PDF	Portable Document Format, a file format created by Adobe™ widely used as a mechanism for publishing documentation.
Product	The item being sold.
Risk analysis	The process of evaluating potential hazards or risks of a product, including inherent hazards, and hazards arising from misuse.
Translation	Process of converting written content in one language into content with the same meaning in another language.
User	A person who uses the product. Also known as the customer or consumer.
Warning	Indicates a hazard with a medium level of risk which, if not avoided, could result in death or serious injury

LIST OF REFERENCES

Authoring Tool Accessibility Guidelines 1.0; W3C Recommendation (2000)

CEN/CENELEC Guide 6 (2003) "Guidelines for Standards developers to address the needs of older persons and persons with disabilities"

Centre de Droit de la Consommation: "The Practical Application of Council Directive 92/59/EEC on General Product Safety" (February 2000)

Council Resolution of 17 December 1998 on operating instructions for technical consumer goods

DIN 2345 (1998): Translation contracts

DIN EN 1070, (1999): Safety of machinery – Terminology; Trilingual version EN 1070: 1998

Directive 73/23/EEC of 19 February 1973 on the harmonization of the laws of Member States relating to electrical equipment designed for use within certain voltage limits

Directive 85/374/EEC of 25 July 1985 of the approximation of the laws, regulations and administrative provisions of the Member States concerning liability for defective products

Directive 87/404/EEC of the European Council of 25 June 1987 on the harmonization of the laws of the Member States relating to simple pressure vessels

Directive 88/378/EEC of 3 May 1988 on the approximation of the laws of the Member States concerning the safety of toys

Directive 89/106/EEC of the European Council of 21 December 1988 on the approximation of laws, regulations and administrative provisions of the Member States relating to construction products

Directive 89/336/EEC of 3 May 1989 on the approximation of the laws of the Member States relating to electromagnetic compatibility

Directive 89/686/EEC of 21 December 1989 on the approximation of the laws of the Member States relating to personal protective equipment

Directive 90/384/EEC of the European Council of 20 June 1990 on the harmonization of the laws of the Member States relating to non-automatic weighing instruments

Directive 90/385/EEC of the European Council of 20 June 1990 on the approximation of the laws of the Member States relating to active implantable medical devices

Directive 92/59/EEC of 29 June 1992 on general product safety

Directive 93/42/EEC of the European Council of 14 June 1993 concerning medical devices

Directive 94/25/EC of the European Parliament and the Council of 16 June 1994 on the approximation of the laws, regulations and administrative provisions of the Member States relating to recreational craft

Directive 94/9/EC of the European Parliament and the Council of 23 March 1994 on the approximation of the laws of the Member States concerning equipment and protective systems intended for use in potentially explosive atmospheres

Directive 95/16/EC of the European Parliament and the Council of 29 June 1995 on the approximation of the laws of the Member States relating to lifts

Directive 97/23/EC of the European Parliament and the Council of 29 May 1997 on the approximation of the laws of the Member States concerning pressure equipment

List of references

Directive 98/37/EC of the European Parliament and the Council of 22 June 1998 on the approximation of the laws of the Member States relating to machinery

Directive 98/79/EC of the European Parliament and the Council of 27 October 1998 on in vitro diagnostic medical devices

Directive 99/44/EC of the European Parliament and of the Council of 25 May 1999 on certain aspects of the sale of consumer goods and associated guarantees

Directive 99/5/EC of the European Parliament and the Council of 9 March 1999 on radio equipment and telecommunications terminal equipment and the mutual recognition of their conformity

Directive 2000/9/EC of the European Parliament and the Council of 20 March 2000 relating to cable-way installations designed to carry persons

Directive 2001/95/EC of the European Parliament and the Council of 3 December 2001 on general product safety (to be transposed into national legislation by 15 January 2004)

Draft ÖNORM D 1210 (2003): Requirements for technical communication and documentation services

EN 292-2 section 5.5

IEC 62079 Preparation of instructions, Structuring, contents and presentation

ISO 11684 (1995) Tractors, machinery for agriculture and forestry, powered lawn and garden equipment – Safety signs and hazard pictorials – General principles

ISO 12200 (1999): Computer applications in terminology – Machine-readable terminology interchange format (MARTIF)

ISO 704 (2000): Terminology work – Principles and methods

ISO 1087-1 (2000): Terminology work – Vocabulary – Part 1: Theory and application

ISO 1087-2 (2000): Terminology work – Vocabulary - Part 2: Computer applications

ISO 3864-1 (2002) Graphical symbols – Safety colours and safety signs – Part 1: Design principles for safety signs in workplaces

ISO 7010 (2003) Graphical symbols – Safety colours and safety signs – Safety signs used in workplaces and public areas

ISO 12620 (2003): Computer applications in terminology – Data categories

ISO/IEC FDIS 18019 Software and system engineering – Guidelines for the design and preparation of user documentation for applicable software

ÖNORM D 1200 (2000): Translation and Interpretation Services - Requirements for the service and the provision of the service

ÖNORM D 1201 (2000): Translation and Interpretation Services – Translation contracts

Ralf Geyer, tekom Hochschulschriften 4: Evaluation von Gebrauchsanleitungen, 2000

Report of the EC-Commission dated 31 January 2001 about the application of Directive 85/374/EEC on liability for defective products (KOM (2000) 893)

User Agent Accessibility Guidelines 1.0; W3C Recommendation (2002)

Web Content Accessibility Guidelines 1.0; W3C Recommendation (1999)

XML Accessibility Guidelines; W3C Working draft (2002)

USEFUL LINKS

Directives
- http://www.newapproach.org/Directives/Default.asp
- http://europa.eu.int/eur-lex/
- http://europa.eu.int/comm/enterprise/newapproach/index.htm
- EU legislation related to consumer product safety:
  http://europa.eu.int/comm/consumers/cons_safe/prod_safe/other_EU/cons_prod_en.htm
- Directive 2001/95/EC:
  http://europa.eu.int/comm/consumers/cons_safe/prod_safe/gpsd/revisedGPSD_en.htm
- Directive 99/44/EC:
  http://europa.eu.int/comm/consumers/cons_int/safe_shop/guarantees/index_en.htm
- Directive 92/59/EEC:
  http://europa.eu.int/comm/consumers/cons_safe/prod_safe/gpsd/index_en.htm
- Directive 85/374/EEC:
  http://europa.eu.int/comm/consumers/cons_safe/prod_safe/defect_prod/index_en.htm

Council Resolutions
- Council Resolution of 17 December 1998 on operating instructions for technical consumer goods:
  http://europa.eu.int/eur-lex/pri/en/oj/dat/1998/c_411/c_41119981231en00010004.pdf

Accessibility
- http://www.w3.org/WAI/Resources/#gl

European Standards Bodies
- CEN - European Committee for Standardization
  http://www.cenorm.org/cenorm/index.htm
- CENELEC - European Committee for Electrotechnical Standardization
  http://www.cenelec.org/Cenelec/Homepage.htm
- ETSI - European Telecommunications Standards Institute
  http://www.etsi.org/aboutetsi/home.htm

International Standards Bodies
- International Organization for Standardization
  http://www.iso.org/iso/en/ISOOnline.openerpage

National Standards Bodies

Austria: Österreichisches Normungsinstitut
Heinestraße 38
1020 Wien
Email: sales@on-norm.at
Phone: +43-1-21300-805
Fax: +43-1-21300-815
http://www.oenorm.at

Useful Links

Belgium:
Institut belge de normalisation (IBN) /
Belgisch Instituut voor Normalisatie (BIN)
avenue de la Brabançonne, 29
1000 Bruxelles
Phone: +32-2-738 01 11
Fax: +32-2-733 42 64
Email: info@ibn.be
http://www.ibn.be

Czech Republic:
Èeský normalizaèní institut
Biskupský dvùr 5
110 02 PRAHA 1
Phone: +42-221-802 111
Fax: +42-221-802 301
Email: info@csni.cz
http://www.csni.cz

Denmark:
Dansk Standard
Kollegievej 6
2920 Charlottenlund
Phone: +45-39-96 61 01
Fax: +45-39-96 61 02
Email: dansk.standard@ds.dk
http://www.ds.dk

Finland:
Suomen Standardisoimisliitto SFS Ry
Maistraatinportti 2
00240 Helsinki
Email: sfs@sfs.fi
Phone: +358-9-149 9331
Fax: +358-9-146 4925
http://www.sfs.fi

France:
Association Française de Normalisation
11, avenue Francis de Pressensé
93571 Saint-Denis La Plaine Cedex
Phone: +33-1-41 62 80 00
Fax: +33-1-49 17 90 00
http://www.afnor.fr

Germany:
DIN Deutsches Institut für Normung e. V.
Burggrafenstraße 6
10787 Berlin
Phone: +49-30-26010
Fax: +49-30-2601 1260
E-Mail: postmaster@din.de
http://www2.din.de

Useful Links

Greece: Hellenic Organization for Standardization
 313 Acharnon Str.
 111 45, Athens, GREECE
 Phone: +30-210-2120100
 Fax: +30-210-228 3034
 Email: info@elot.gr
 http://www.elot.gr

Hungary: Magyar Szabványügyi Testület
 1091 Budapest Üllői út 25.
 Phone: +36-1-4566800
 Fax: +36-1-4566823
 Email: msztinfo@mszt.hu
 http://www.mszt.hu

Iceland: IST – Stadlaráð Íslands
 Laugavegur 178
 IS-105 Reykjavik
 Phone: +354-520-7150
 Fax: +354-520-7171
 Email: stadlar@stadlar.is
 http://www.stadlar.is

Ireland: NSAI – National Standards Authority of Ireland
 Glasnevin,
 Dublin 9
 Phone: +353-1-8073800
 Fax: +353-1-8073838
 Email: nsai@nsai.ie
 http://www.nsai.ie/Home/Home_Page/index.html

Italy: UNI – Ente Nazionale Italiano di Unificazione
 Sede di Milano
 via Battistotti Sassi 11B
 20133 MILANO MI
 Phone: +39-02-700241
 Email: uni@uni.com
 http://www.uni.com

Luxembourg: SEE - Organisme Luxembourgeois de Normalisation
 see.normalisation@eg.etat.lu
 http://www.etat.lu/SEE/normalisation.htm

Netherlands: Nederlands Normalisatie-instituut
 Postbus 5059
 2600 GB Delft
 Phone: +31-15-2 690 390
 Fax: +31-15-2 690 190
 http://www.nen.nl

Useful Links

Norway:	Standard Norge Pronorm AS Postboks 252 1326 Lysaker Phone: +47-67-83 87 00 Fax: +47-67-83 87 01 Email: pronorm@standard.no http://www.standard.no
Poland:	Polski Komtet Normalizacyjny http://www.pkn.pl
Portugal:	Instituto Português da Qualidade Phone: +351-21-294 81 02 Fax: +351-21-294 82 23 Email: spr@mail.ipq.pt http://www.ipq.pt
Slovakia:	Slovenský ústav technickej normalizácie Karloveská 63 P.O. BOX 246 840 00 Bratislava, SLOVAKIA Phone: +421-2-6029 4474 Fax: +421-2-6541 1888 Email: ms_post@sutn.gov.sk http://www.sutn.gov.sk
Spain:	Asociación Española de Normalización y Certificación Génova, 6 28004 MADRID Phone: +34-914-32 60 00 Fax: +34-913 10 40 32 Email: aenor@aenor.es http://www.aenor.es
Sweden:	SIS Sankt Paulsgatan 6 118 80 STOCKHOLM Phone: +46-8-555 520 00 Fax: +46-8-555 520 01 Email: Info@sis.se http://www.sis.se
Switzerland:	Schweizerische Normen-Vereinigung Bürglistr. 29 8400 Winterthur Phone: +41-52-224 54 54 Fax: +41-52-224 54 74 info@snv.ch http://www.snv.ch/

Useful Links

United Kingdom: BSI British Standards HQ
389 Chiswick High Road
London
W4 4AL
United Kingdom
Phone: +44-20-8996 9000
Fax: +44-20-8996 7001
Email: cservices@bsi-global.com
http://www.bsi-global.com

European organisations for Technical Communication

Denmark: Dantekom
toc@foss-electric.dk

Finland: Suomen Tekniset Dokumentoijat ry
http://www.dokumentoijat.net/

France: Conseil des Rédacteurs Techniques
crt@conseil.org
http://www.chez.com/crt/

Germany: tekom Gesellschaft für technische Kommunikation e.V.
info@tekom.de
http://www.tekom.de

Great Britain: Institute of Scientific and Technical Communicators
istc@istc.org.uk
http://www.istc.org.uk

Netherlands: Studiekring voor Technische Informatie en Communicatie
c.jansen@let.kun.nl
http://www.stic.nl

Spain: Tecom España
info@tecom-es.org
http://www.tecom-es.org/

Sweden: Föreningen Teknisk Information
info@fti.org.se
http://www.fti.org.se/

Switzerland: Tecom Schweiz
info@tecom.ch
http://www.tecom.ch/

Europe: TCeurope
info@tceurope.org
http://www.tceurope.org

www.ingramcontent.com/pod-product-compliance
Ingram Content Group UK Ltd.
Pitfield, Milton Keynes, MK11 3LW, UK
UKHW051523180426
11947UKWH00018B/1548